# THE ROAD TO RUNNYMEDE

*The Medieval Saga Series*
*Book Six*

**David Field**

*Also in the Medieval Saga Series*

Conquest

Traitor's Arrow

An Uncivil War

The Lion of Anjou

The Absentee King

The Conscience of a King

# THE ROAD TO RUNNYMEDE

Published by Sapere Books.

24 Trafalgar Road, Ilkley, LS29 8HH,
United Kingdom

saperebooks.com



ISBN: 978-1-80055-901-1

# I

It was late March 1194, and those seated around the table in the Great Hall of Nottingham Castle were bent upon restoring England to a permanent state of peace. King Richard was in the centre, with his elderly mother Eleanor, now in her seventy-second year, to his right, and the newly appointed Justiciar Hubert Walter to his left. The remainder of the hastily assembled Council were there because they could each, in their own way, contribute to the restoration process by virtue of either their talents or their vast landholdings.

Among those who brought military skill and unswerving loyalty to the table was Hugh, Earl of Flint — a title he'd inherited from his father-in-law, whom he had never met. His wife Edwina, as the deceased earl's only child, was the heiress to the estate, but Hugh would have been granted a similar title even without his wife, given his tried and tested sword arm and his fearless service to Richard, King of England. Hugh had first fought during the three-year Crusade that had been waged in order to re-open Jerusalem to Christian pilgrims. More recently, he'd served during the siege of the castle in which they now sat, the last stronghold of Richard's errant younger brother John, now skulking somewhere in France, having abandoned his erstwhile supporters to their fates.

The Council was now meeting in order to determine those fates. Before business commenced, Richard leaned forward to speak to Hugh. 'How fares your father?'

'Middling well, sire,' Hugh replied, grateful for the king's solicitude. His father William was at least still in the land of the living, although seriously weakened by his sufferings as a prisoner in this very castle. He'd been held underground without food or water in one of the dungeon caves set into its sandstone rock base. William's jailor had been the wicked sheriff left in command of the castle by the would-be usurper Prince John, and the rescue had been masterminded by William's other son, Robert, who ran the family estate of Repton, a half day's ride to the west. Robert had been assisted by a ragged army of landless 'outlaws' — victims of the sheriff's cruel policies of eviction and persecution.

'And your mother?' Queen Eleanor asked. 'Does she minister to his needs, as she once so faithfully ministered to mine?'

'Indeed, Your Majesty,' Hugh replied. 'She remains forever grateful for your generosity in allowing her to be by his side as he regains his strength.'

He was not merely being sycophantic. His mother Adele had been Eleanor's Senior Lady since the days when she had been married to the former King Henry. She had loyally and uncomplainingly followed the now ageing queen dowager throughout the Plantagenet lands across the Channel, separated from her husband, Hugh's father, for many months at a time. Adele had been allowed leave of absence from Court to remain on the Repton estate for as long as William needed her. Hugh was hoping that this was merely a prelude to her being replaced entirely as Senior Lady, allowing her a few years of peaceful retirement.

Hugh's wishes were inspired by more than filial concern, since his own wife Edwina was also a Senior Lady, in her case to the continually absent Queen Berengaria, wife of King Richard, who seemed to prefer the softer life, food and weather of Anjou. Berengaria therefore required her constant attendant to foreswear the comfort of home, whether it was on the Repton estate of her in-laws, or the estate in Flintshire, on the border of Wales, of which she was now the countess. For the moment Edwina was in Repton with their son Geoffrey, born in Tyre during the Crusading days in Outremer.

'I trust that your father will soon be able to resume his duties?' Hubert Walter asked of Hugh. 'In my role as Justiciar, I shall require the advice and experience of a Chief Justice of his calibre. Prince John did the nation no service when he dismissed William from office, and praise be to God for inspiring His Majesty to reinstate him.'

Given that Walter was also the Archbishop of Canterbury, in addition to holding the twin offices of Justiciar and Chancellor, his reference to Richard having been inspired by God was a double compliment. However, the king gave a word of caution on behalf of William, who was now only a few months short of his seventieth birthday.

'Do not urge him back into office before he has fully recovered from his dreadful ordeal, Hubert,' he told his Justiciar. 'He has proved himself time and again to be inclined to ignore his own health in the service of the nation, and I would not wish this devotion to be the cause of his demise.'

'I seem to recall hearing my mother saying something similar not a week ago,' Hugh said.

The king continued to gaze down the table at Hugh. 'You have yet to visit your new estate by the River Dee?'

'Indeed, sire, since I have only been its earl for less than a week.'

Richard nodded towards the man three seats down from Eleanor. 'And there sits the man to whom you must pledge fealty. There is no time like the present, as our country cousins are wont to say.'

Hugh looked down the table at Ranulf de Blondeville, the young man eleven years his junior, who had acquired the title of Earl of Chester at the age of eleven. He had only recently come into his majority as one of the most powerful barons in the land, with vast estates in the north-west of England.

Like many who now held the balance of power around the throne, he was also well connected to France. Conscious of the need to keep such magnates close to him, King Richard had, four years previously, ordered Ranulf to marry Duchess Constance of Brittany, the widow of Richard's older brother Geoffrey and the mother of Arthur of Brittany, who'd been declared as Richard's successor to the crown of England. Not only were Richard and Ranulf thereby united by marriage, but when Ranulf's stepson Arthur inherited the English throne the already powerful Earl of Chester would be pre-eminent among the English barons.

The homage ceremony was conducted briefly, and Eleanor whispered urgently in Richard's ear that they had important affairs of State to dispose of.

'Indeed we do,' Richard confirmed. 'I suppose we must begin with the matter of my wayward brother.'

The king was referring to Prince John's many misdeeds, committed while he and Eleanor had been abroad. Richard had spent much of his reign on Crusade, after which he'd been kidnapped by Duke Leopold of Austria. This had wrung a ransom of one hundred and fifty thousand marks from his subjects, a taxation process that still rankled with many of those nobles who had, by virtue of the size of their estates, been required to pay the most.

John had used Richard's enforced absence from the realm to undermine his older brother's authority, casting doubt on his honour, his integrity, and his military prowess. He had also imposed further extortionate taxes, not so much on the nobles whose support he needed, but on the tradesman and peasant classes. He evicted tenants who could not pay and subjected them to barbaric and inhuman punishments when they stole deer and other livestock from the royal forests in order to save their families from starvation. His henchmen in this process had been the sheriffs of the various counties, many of whom were on the list in front of Justiciar Walter, awaiting judgment for their part in the malicious policies that had cost so many lives.

'Perhaps we *should* begin with your brother,' Hubert Walter conceded tentatively, 'since it was for obeying his commands that so many now stand condemned for their vile and cruel atrocities.'

'Not on his command as such,' Eleanor insisted. 'Let us rather say "by virtue of his lax management of affairs".'

Everyone held their breath and awaited Richard's response. It was to be expected that even now Dowager Queen Eleanor would seek some form of absolution and forgiveness for her youngest son, and it remained to be seen how Richard would respond. He frowned as he turned his face towards his mother's.

'I would be more inclined to give my brother the benefit of the doubt were it not for the fact that he fled the realm before my return, has ever sought support and military assistance from our French enemies, and has not seen fit to face me and seek my forgiveness.'

'He is perhaps afraid that you will have him condemned for treason and done to death,' Eleanor observed. 'I know that you are better than that, Richard, but ever since your nursery days you have played the bully towards him. His actions during your absence from England cannot be condoned, but it is arguable that they were intended to preserve your throne until your return.'

'I would rather hear that pathetic excuse from his own lips than from behind the skirts of our mother,' Richard replied grimly. 'When I hunt him down, I shall ask him to his face what he thought he was about during my absence. The nation was held in the grip of fear for four long years, and the image of Plantagenet has been forever besmirched. Our father — your dear late husband — is no doubt turning in his grave at what has become of our once noble family name.'

There were silent nods from around the table, although no one dared voice an opinion that would offend either the king or the mother who he still held in high esteem. It was Justiciar Walter who steered the business back onto its proper course.

'Given that it would perhaps be best for the royal brothers to resolve any differences they may have face to face, we might instead proceed with the fates of those whose hands are stained with so much blood, however misguidedly they may have interpreted their orders?'

Since John's fate had yet to be decided, there was no yardstick against which to judge the actions of those who had — whatever his tolerant mother might think — acted simply on his orders. Fearful that if banishment were imposed upon them, thus by comparison suggesting worse for John himself, the Council opted for those named on the list to be fined heavily, with loss of estates as the penalty for default. It then went on to call upon John, by proclamation, to present himself at Winchester by the end of May at the latest, and to forfeit his remaining estates if he did not. Finally it imposed a carucage tax on all estates, based on the estimated value of all landholdings. This was intended to finance Richard's planned return across the Channel to seek the repossession of those lands claimed by England that had been seized by Philip of France during the uncertainty of recent times.

Before rising and inviting the Council members to join him for dinner, Richard announced that he required his leading magnates to assemble their forces and gather in Winchester ahead of reprisal attacks on the French king. Hugh nodded, while mentally noting that this gave him several weeks in which to set his affairs in order.

'But I have no skill in arms, sire,' Ranulf of Chester protested.

'Of this I am well aware, Ranulf, but you possess something of arguably greater value — namely your family connections with those currently close to the throne of France,' Richard said reassuringly.

Ranulf's face grew pale at the prospect of finally confronting the divided loyalties that encumbered the two de Montfort family estates on either side of the Vexin border with the Île-de-France, but he nodded his agreement nevertheless. The Council members rose and made their way into the side chamber, where dinner awaited them.

Hugh took the opportunity to delay Ranulf briefly by plucking at his tunic sleeve. 'Now that you are my liege lord, you may count upon my men joining your ranks, in addition to my constant presence by your side, ensuring that you are free to conduct such diplomacy as His Majesty shall require of you.'

Ranulf smiled in gratitude. 'I was hoping for such,' he replied, 'and you may in turn rely upon my constant support for whatever you may have in mind on your estates.'

'Estates that I must hasten to visit for the first time,' Hugh replied, lowering his voice, 'before I am once more dragged across the Channel in the seemingly endless squabble between men who are brothers only by birth.'

The first estate Hugh visited was barely a two-hour ride to the west, and it was the one he had left at daybreak in order to attend the Council meeting. He found his father William crouched over a roaring fire in the Great Hall of Repton Manor House, wrapped in horse blankets that, despite several fastidious washings, still smelled faintly of their previous occupants. Although it was now fully spring, and the daytime air was warm, the fire had been stacked high with timber, and the room was over-hot. Despite that, William was still shivering as he raised his head to greet Hugh.

'How went matters in Nottingham?'

'Middling well, Father. Mother will no doubt be displeased to learn that you are still the Chief Justice of England.'

'When does King Richard require me to resume my duties?'

'Once you are fully recovered, and not before. You are lucky to be alive after your ordeal — few men could have survived being locked in a prison cell within the castle rock and deprived of food and water for a week.'

'Nor would I have done, without the timely intervention of your brother and his friends from the Shire Wood. Have you thanked him sufficiently?'

'Of course, Father. He may be many years younger than me, but I recognise in him the same boldness that has sustained me so well in the royal service — though perhaps not in such an elevated office as yours, nor even Mother's. It is to be hoped that Queen Eleanor honours her pledge to free her of further duties until you are back to your old self.'

'I fear that I will never be,' William muttered as he shivered yet again. 'This ague seems reluctant to leave me, and yet Robert advises that the crops have begun to shoot in the home meadow, and that the summer is but weeks away. If I am not recovered by next winter, I fear the worst.'

'All the more reason for consuming this beef tea,' came the stern instruction from Adele, Countess of Repton, and Hugh's mother, who had followed him into the chamber. Although in her mid-sixties she was still hale and hearty, and kept active by the need to ensure that her beloved husband of over thirty years did what he was told by his physician.

William grimaced as he took the steaming mug from her hand and sniffed its contents. 'Was the cow from which this was concocted dead at the time?'

'At least you have not lost your sense of humour,' came another familiar voice from the doorway. Hugh's wife Edwina — now Countess of Flint — stood there with her precious bundle. 'I've brought your grandson to supervise the taking of your physic,' she added as little Geoffrey gurgled.

William smiled. 'I see that I have no option, but is this all that I am to be offered for my dinner? Robert advises me that they shot a deer in the home coppice, and I was hopeful of venison.'

'That will be ready by the time you drink up your beef tea like a wise man,' Hugh said as he walked over to Edwina and Geoffrey, giving them each a kiss as he made for the door.

He wandered outside, where his brother Robert sat on a stool, shaping a bow. Robert's wife, Beth, scuttled around the yard, ensuring that their son Thomas didn't fall into the dust as he staggered on infant legs with all the grace of a newborn colt.

There was a fifteen-year age gap between the two brothers, who had only met for the first time shortly before their father had been unjustly confined within Nottingham Castle. Nevertheless there was an unspoken bond between them, in addition to a marked physical similarity.

'How goes Father today?' Robert asked as baby Thomas crumpled into the dust for the third time.

Hugh frowned. 'Little has changed. If this ague doesn't lift soon, I fear the worst for him at summer's end. Then you will become Earl of Repton.'

'You know I do not wish it, Hugh,' Robert assured him yet again. 'If you prefer, I will gladly renounce it in your favour, as the older brother. That *is* the law, after all.'

'It may be the law,' Hugh said, 'but it is not natural justice. Besides which I have a larger estate that I have yet to visit. We shall take our leave the day after tomorrow, and I leave Father's welfare in your capable hands.'

'Rest assured that I will take great care of him,' Robert replied, 'always assuming that I can get past Mother. I only hope that Beth will be prepared to take such good care of me should I be similarly afflicted.'

'I would wish the same for myself, at Edwina's kindly hand,' Hugh replied as he looked back towards the manor house. 'But it is long past the day when I should have taken her home.'

The Flint estate seemed to shimmer in the reflected sunlight from the broad Dee Estuary as Hugh and Edwina trotted their horses through the gates. Young Geoffrey was sleeping contentedly in the crook of his mother's arm.

As they approached, a figure emerged from the manor house and a matronly voice called out, 'May the saints be praised! Is that my own little "Weena" back to comfort me in my old age?'

'God bless you, Nan,' Edwina cried as she was lifted down from her palfrey by Hugh. He took Geoffrey from her and stood by with an indulgent smile as the portly middle-aged lady embraced his wife and let loose a flood of tears.

Edwina disentangled herself from what threatened to become an endless embrace and turned to indicate Hugh with an outstretched arm. 'Meet the new Earl of Flint, Nan — my husband Hugh, a trusted knight in the immediate retinue of His Majesty King Richard. You also have a new child to drool over, as you once did me. His name is Geoffrey, and he is almost walking.'

Nan held out her experienced arms for her new charge, and cooed happily as she admired his rosy cheeks.

Edwina turned to Hugh. 'As you will have deduced for yourself, "Nan" here was my childhood nurse. I thank the good offices of the steward that she has not been dismissed now that my parents are no more.'

Nan's face fell. 'Your father's passing was sudden, Mistress. Not like your mother's, all those years ago, who suffered so dreadfully in her final weeks.'

'No more of that, Nan.' Edwina shuddered at the memories that this brought back. 'And please do not feel obliged to call me "Mistress". To you I was always "Weena" — the name you taught me — and "Weena" I shall always be to you. I shall leave it to you to call Geoffrey whatever you wish, and if you bring him up as well as you did me, then I shall have no fears about leaving him in your care.'

'You are leaving so soon?' Nan asked in alarm, but Edwina shook her head.

'Not for several weeks, but then we are bound back into the royal service, each in our own way. I am Senior Lady to Queen Berengaria, who has yet to visit our shores, and when Hugh crosses the Channel in King Richard's throng, I shall accompany him in order to resume my duties. But until then I am free to teach Hugh how to fish in the river.'

The weeks passed all too quickly. In mid-May Hugh felt the familiar weight of heavy armour on his shoulders, and the reassuring rolling rump of his favourite courser, Atlas, as he processed down the greensward that lay outside the gates of Winchester Castle, two paces behind King Richard, in the front rank of his Household Guard. Prince John had not presented himself as commanded, and they were now bound across the water to hunt him down, while reclaiming for England those lands that were traditionally part of the Plantagenet empire.

# II

It was hot and sticky on the quayside at Barfleur as the royal party began the slow process of unloading, but at least the sea crossing was over, and hopefully Edwina would now stop throwing up. It had been the roughest crossing Hugh could remember, and his wife had retained her fear of the sea ever since she'd been shipwrecked on the voyage out to Outremer, so all in all it was time to give thanks to God for a safe delivery. However, they would soon be parted, and Hugh was still asking himself why.

There was an obvious reason why *he* was here, supervising the unloading of men and horses from the vessels that tied up behind their own, and preparing them for the march south-east to Caen. Philip of France, ever the opportunist, had taken advantage of Richard's brief return to England in order to make territorial gains, and much of Normandy east of the mighty Seine had fallen to his advancing army. He was last heard of laying siege to Verneuil, on the south-western bank of the river that divided the south of Normandy from east to west. Given its proximity to Paris, it was strategically important to whoever held its castle.

Richard had issued orders that his forces were to lose no time in marching south-east from Barfleur, by way of Caen, in order to drive Philip back from where he had come. However, Hugh had been hoping that first they would head south-west into Anjou, and in particular to the royal palace at Beaufort-en-Vallée. Even if Richard had no wish to spend time with his wife, at least this would give Hugh a few more nights with his.

Queen Berengaria had yet to set foot in England, and had even declined to attend the recent ceremony in Winchester during which Richard had been recrowned by Archbishop of Canterbury Hubert Walter in order to erase the stigma of his lengthy imprisonment. There were rumours that she and Richard were no longer the loving couple that romantic balladeers had flattered in song, and the rumours would only be strengthened if Richard continued east in pursuit of Philip of France, rather than be reunited with his queen.

Richard had insisted that Edwina join the voyage to Barfleur, ostensibly to act as Senior Lady to his ageing mother Eleanor in the absence of her usual Lady, Hugh's mother Adele. It was also held to be beyond argument that once Eleanor had been safely delivered to her preferred residence in the Abbey of Fontevrault, only a gentle two-day ride from Beaufort, Edwina was to return to service in the household of Queen Berengaria. Hugh, on the other hand, was required to give further life-risking service in the front line of Richard's forces as they sought to regain supremacy in Normandy.

As if to emphasise his desire to bypass his own wife by the widest route possible, Richard, with Eleanor borne in a litter in the centre of the vanguard of the huge progress, travelled via Bayeux and Caen — with an overnight rest in each town — to Lisieux, where word was sent down the line that they were to rest for several days. Hugh was more than puzzled by the seemingly inordinate delay in what should have been a hasty, almost forced, march south-east to prevent Philip of France from acquiring any more of Normandy. He was also enquiring loudly, of all around him, why Eleanor had not already turned south, but Edwina bade him keep his thoughts to himself.

'Queen Eleanor herself has ordered that we journey here, and has refused to disclose the reason for it even to King

Richard. If she will not even tell her own son what she is about, then she is hardly likely to disclose it to others. All I know is that I am to lay out her finest Court gowns for at least two nights.'

The reason for the subterfuge became glaringly apparent two nights later, as they sat at supper in the house of John, Archdeacon of Lisieux. A page entered stealthily by the rear door of the chamber, walking past the table at which Hugh and Edwina were seated in case their services were required by either Richard or Eleanor. He then made his way to the top table, where he whispered in the archdeacon's ear. The clergyman turned to Richard and announced, 'Sire, there is a penitent without who seeks the royal forgiveness and the kiss of eternal peace.'

'I am still at supper, as you can see for yourself,' Richard replied testily. 'Can the matter not wait?'

'When a man wishes to make peace with his conscience, it ill behoves any Christian — least of all such a powerful Christian ruler as yourself — to stand in the way of that, Richard,' Eleanor told him with a stern countenance. 'Let the man be admitted.'

'Very well,' Richard grudgingly agreed as he went back to his dish of salmon, only raising his head and looking round when he heard the gasps of those around him.

In the rear doorway, on his knees, with tears streaming down his face, knelt a man who was familiar to Hugh by sight, but with whom he had never conversed. He held his breath as he felt Edwina's trembling hand clutching his sleeve, and they waited to see how this encounter might unfold.

'Dearest brother,' the man wept through choking breaths, 'I seek only your forgiveness and brotherly clemency for the wickedness of my past years. I wish, ere I die, to be reunited with the companion of my nursery, the joint heir to our father's seed and our mother's womb. Take me back into your bosom, dearest brother, and I will serve you in whatever humbled capacity you shall see fit. Or take my life, should you deem it appropriate. Grant me only the blessing of knowing that I am forgiven.'

Richard's face drained of all the ruddy colour it normally displayed as he dropped his eating knife, rose from his seat and approached the man. He was followed closely by Eleanor, who waved Edwina back into her seat as she rose in order to assist her. She stepped between the kneeling man and the son who stood looking down at him with a tear forming in the corner of one eye, then reached out, took each of their hands and clasped them together.

'It was your father's dying wish that the two of you be united in brotherly love for the good of Anjou and all the other estates he ruled. For the love of God, Richard, show some compassion to your little brother.'

'I am not worthy of anything other than a traitor's grave,' John wheedled, 'yet I would go to it happier knowing that you have restored your love to my pathetic self, even though I have done you grievous wrong, of which I now bitterly repent me.'

Richard reached out with both hands, lifted John to his feet, and with a voice breaking with emotion he replied, 'Think no more of it, John. You are but a child, and were left to evil counsellors. Your advisers shall pay for this. Now, come and have something to eat.'

An extra chair was hastily summoned and placed next to Richard's. He slid the largely untouched salmon dish in front of John and sent word to the kitchen to bring more without delay.

'Archdeacon John reached across and handed Richard the basket loaded with bread slices. 'Loaves and fishes will suffice equally well in the absence of a fatted calf, I think,' he suggested.

The following morning Hugh was summoned to the main room of the archdeacon's residence that was serving as the royal audience chamber. He found John seated beside King Richard, along with Walter de Coutances, Archbishop of Rouen, and William de Longchamp, recently reinstated as Chancellor of England, both of whom had made the Channel crossing with Richard. Standing behind them all was the man known only as 'Mercadier', a fierce mercenary leader who had been at Richard's side ever since his return from the Crusade, and who was the most feared warrior in southern territories such as Limoges and Toulouse. Hugh felt his hopes rising as he speculated that Mercadier would be the one chosen as Richard's personal bodyguard in what was to follow, so he bowed silently and kept his head down until spoken to. Instead, he found himself being spoken *about*.

'John,' Richard announced breezily, 'allow me to introduce Hugh, Earl of Flint by my hand. He is one of my trusted captains, and his father is William, Earl of Repton and Chief Justice of England.'

'The father I have met,' John replied enigmatically, as he recalled the arrogant lawyer he'd yelled at while resident in Nottingham Castle some years previously, 'but not the son. I shall enjoy making his further acquaintance as we battle Philip of France.'

'For Hugh, that is a pleasure that must be delayed,' Richard announced. 'It will be his first mission to escort our mother to her preferred residence in the Abbey of Fontevrault, after first leaving his beautiful wife, the Countess Edwina, to attend upon the Queen at Beaufort-en-Vallée. Then he will rejoin us at wherever we shall prove to be, hopefully within sight of Paris. Hugh, you should know that my brother John brings to me not only renewed hopes that we may henceforth live as true brothers, but also various estates in Normandy that he had previously held of Philip of France. Since they were my estates in the first place, he experiences a brotherly desire to offer them back to me without the consent of the French idiot. One of these is Évreux, in the Vexin, where hopefully we shall meet up once you have conveyed the ladies to their new residences and once I have sent Philip back to his smelly goat hut alongside the pestilential Seine.'

'And your personal safety during that progress?' Hugh asked with a meaningful glance at Mercadier.

'You and Mercadier have fought alongside each other for long enough for you to rest assured that he will be more than capable of guarding my person as we take back Normandy.'

Hugh nodded towards Mercadier. 'For myself, I would not wish anyone else to be at my back on the field of battle.'

'Good, so that is settled,' Richard concluded as he called for wine. 'Let us drink to *our* success, and Philip's damnation.'

What followed more closely resembled a game of armed chess than a war. Philip of France had been unsuccessfully laying siege to Verneuil, on the western banks of the Seine. Its location within the Île-de-France that was the traditional French stronghold made its occupation by English men at arms not only an insult to French pride, but also a threat to morale.

Richard rode hard to relieve the siege, with Mercadier by his side, and had the satisfaction of seeing Philip's forces disperse in disarray at the sight of the mighty English horde bearing down on them. The French then hastily reassembled and proceeded down the long valley of the Loire, seeking to cut Normandy off from the rest of the English estates in Anjou and further south. They were pursued every mile of the way by a fast force led by Mercadier until they reached Fréteval, where Philip learned, to his horror, that further English forces under the Earl of Flint were waiting for them on the north bank of the river.

Hugh had chosen the fastest route from Beaufort-en-Vallée, having bade a tearful farewell to Edwina. He could hardly believe his good fortune when he saw the French battle pennants flying in the stiff wind blowing across the Loire, and learned from forward scouts who had skirted to the east that the main English force under Mercadier was moving west in pursuit of Philip's marauding army.

Caught in a classic pincer movement, Philip gathered his closest advisers round him and opted to flee, leaving most of his baggage behind. Demoralised by their leader's flight, the French troops made a disorderly withdrawal, many of them slaughtered by Mercadier's men as they fled east. Richard withdrew all of his forces to nearby Le Mans.

Despatches were awaiting them there, and among them was a letter from Hubert Walter, left behind to govern England while Richard and his other advisers were hastily winning back the lands lost to Philip. It was addressed to Hugh, and conveyed the sad news that his father William had passed away as the first of the autumn mists wrapped the Repton estate in its chilly folds. Hugh was sitting quietly in a pew to the front of the nave in the Cathedral of St Julian, praying for his late father's soul, and wondering how his mother was enduring the loss of her dearly beloved husband, when a heavy mailed hand landed on his shoulder. He spun round, instinctively reaching towards his sword hilt. Then he blushed and begged forgiveness when he realised that he had been about to draw his weapon in the presence of King Richard.

'I would have done the same,' Richard said, 'and I apologise for intruding upon your grief. Walter has just advised me of the death of your father, which is also a great loss to England.'

'You are both kind and generous, sire,' Hugh replied, 'but I have to agree that he was a man like no other. It is too easy for those like myself to take up arms and kill men on the field of battle, but his courage was of the spirit — always fighting for what he believed to be right. It was this that cost him his life.'

'I am well aware of his bravery and staunch support when my foolish brother was led astray by scum such as Sheriff de Wendenal. I shall honour the promise I made to allow your younger brother to succeed to the Earldom of Repton. How will your mother take the loss?'

'Her heart will be broken, sire, and I would dearly love to be by her side, to bring her such comfort as I am able.'

'That is why I sought you out, Hugh. My mother has graciously discharged yours from her service, and granted her a token pension of ten pounds a year. She has no need of the money, clearly, but will hopefully take some comfort from the kindness of her former mistress. I also wish you to cross back over to England with those tidings, and provide her with a shoulder upon which to lean.'

Tears formed in Hugh's eyes as he thanked Richard profusely for his generosity, but the king raised a hand to silence him.

'I am also well reminded of your loyalty to me in the years when I needed every friend I could gather round me. You also saved the life of my mother and my wife during that shipwreck on the voyage to Outremer, and it is only fitting that I repay that favour by bringing such succour as I am able to your own family in its hour of need. Mercadier's skills on the battlefield are such that I shall be able to part with your strong sword arm for a few weeks. After that, I wish you to take up a position equivalent to his within the ranks of my brother John's forces. In the main they lack discipline, and John has asked me to supply him with someone who can kick them into line.'

'Rest assured that I shall not fail him upon my return,' Hugh replied as he rose from his pew and bowed. 'It is true what they say — that England was never so blessed than on the day that Richard Plantagenet took the throne.'

The following day he rode out of Le Mans much lighter of heart. Instead of heading north along the road that led to Barfleur, he took the southern route to Beaufort-en-Vallée, where late on the second day he found Edwina in her tiny private chamber. Her eyes flew open with delight when she saw him in the doorway, then she rushed to his side, wrapping her arms tightly around him and demanding to know the reason for his unexpected visit.

Sadly he explained that William, Earl of Repton was no more, but that he had been granted leave to visit his mother in order to console her as best he could in her grief. 'But I could not leave without seeing you ere I depart on my long journey. Given that we were billeted in le Mans, the opportunity was too tempting.'

'May I not come with you?' Edwina suggested. 'I long to hold little Geoffrey in my arms again.'

'But what of your duties here?' Hugh asked. 'Will Queen Berengaria be likely to grant you leave?'

Edwina's face curdled into an expression of distaste. 'I doubt that she would even notice my absence. Upon my return I found her surrounded by ladies from her own lands, who make a point of insulting me by speaking in their own tongue whenever I am around, then mocking the French language when they deign to address me. I would propose that I depart with you whenever you deem it appropriate, leaving a note with the lowest serving wench advising Her High and Mighty Majesty that I have chosen to resume my role as Countess of Flint.'

Hugh grinned as he held her to him. 'We leave in the morning, perhaps before the sun has risen. Which will, of course, require that we retire early.'

It was a tearful homecoming for several reasons. On the day after their return, Robert sought out Hugh as he leaned on the fence surrounding the piggery, gazing down the slope towards the Manor Wood that supplied so much of the estate's easy wealth by way of timber. This was regularly carted off to the nearby Swarkestone Mill.

'King Richard granted you leave of absence from slaughtering the Frenchies?' Robert asked. 'Or did you simply desert?'

Hugh laughed hollowly. 'You are clearly not a man at arms. Desertion is punishable by death — and desertion from the king's service carries the additional charge of treason, the punishment for which is too horrible to even describe. I was granted leave, but I know not for how long. I must of course ride north to my estate in Flint, leaving you as the new Earl of Repton. But tell me truly — how has Mother taken our father's death? She puts on a brave front, but she must surely grieve.'

'We hear her weeping in the quiet hours of the night,' Robert replied sadly, 'but she has appointed herself as both nurse and tutor to little Thomas. He's a strapping young lad.'

'He will hopefully be a fit companion for Geoffrey in years to come,' Hugh said, 'since there is little between them in age. And should I fall in some future battle, I could wish for no-one better to see to his upbringing than his Uncle Robert.'

'Speak not of such things,' Robert shuddered. 'We sons of Repton are indestructible. But when must you leave?'

'Within a few days,' Hugh told him. 'We bide only for long enough to regain our breath, and bring such comfort as we can to Mother.'

In the event, their intended brief stay at Repton dragged into two weeks. Once they reached Flint, it was as if they had lost the will to cross the Channel ever again. The weeks became months, and the months drifted into years, as increasingly terse and petulant despatches from Walter de Coutances, dictated by Prince John and occasionally King Richard, made their way north by messengers sent by Justiciar Hubert Walter. They all demanded that Hugh return without delay to assume the command of John's forces that had been commissioned by the king, and Hugh ignored them all.

These same despatches all told of Richard's increasing triumphs over the forces of Philip of France, and the recapture by the English of all the lands that had been part of the Angevin empire before the death of King Henry. Dowager Queen Eleanor was now only one step away from a life in holy orders, veiled as a sister of the Convent of Fontevrault and cheering on her sons' successes from the distant sidelines. John had apparently honoured the pledge of allegiance that Hugh had heard him swear. Given the unfailingly good news that was being sent across the Channel, Hugh convinced himself that he was not required back over there.

# III

Hugh and Edwina's son Geoffrey was now a lively six-year-old with a passion for horses. Hardly a day passed without the three of them happily traversing their estate that led down to the banks of the Dee, where they would fish happily, but largely unsuccessfully. They would then ride back for an evening meal in the twilight under the overhanging portico of the manor house.

They were seated there one evening in the spring of 1199, watching the sun disappearing behind the mountain ranges in the centre of neighbouring Wales, when Hugh became aware of a distant dust cloud to the south that heralded the hasty arrival of a messenger. The horseman slowly emerged, and for a moment Hugh fancied that his memory was playing tricks on him. Then, as the man dismounted and threw his horse's reins to the stable boy, it became obvious that Hugh was not deceived, and he rose quickly to welcome Mercadier.

'A thousand welcomes, dear friend!' Hugh said, turning to Edwina as he added, 'Allow me to introduce my wife the countess.'

'No time for that,' Mercadier replied brusquely. 'I come here to warn you, in honour of our long friendship. I must tell you that King Richard is dead, and that you are to be taken up for desertion.'

'How, dead?' Hugh asked, appalled, while Edwina gave a muted scream and ran back into the manor house with a hand over her mouth.

Mercadier grimaced. 'His own arrogance and stupidity, as usual. Even though I was by his side, I could not prevent it.'

Hugh bid him take a seat, and called loudly back to the manor house door for more wine and an extra mug, along with bread and meat for their guest. Mercadier thanked him and lowered himself into the seat vacated by Edwina.

'We were in Limoges, putting down a rebellion by its viscount. For reasons best known to himself — but I suspect out of boredom — Richard ordered that we besiege this piss-pot château at Châlus-Chabrol. He was so contemptuous of its pathetic resistance that he opted — against my fervent advice, mind you — to take a stroll, minus his armour, around the foot of its walls while we were hurling whatever we could find over them. There was an archer on the battlement who clearly found our actions amusing, and was batting away our incoming missiles with what appeared to be a frying pan.'

'A what?' Hugh asked.

'You obviously find that as amusing as Richard did, because he yelled up to the man that he would be better employed using the pan to cook his supper. The man — although in reality he was little more than a boy — put down the pan and produced a crossbow, which he fired, hitting Richard in the shoulder. I took him back to our tent, where a physician removed the bolt, but after a few days it appeared that the wound had festered and grown poisonous. Richard slowly grew weaker, then in the second week he died of the infection. We had his heart sent to Rouen, while his body, at his grieving mother's request, was buried at his father's feet in the Abbey of Fontevrault.'

'What happened to the man who had killed him?' Hugh asked, to a responding snort from Mercadier.

'While he was seemingly marked for death, Richard had the boy brought before him. We had overrun the château on the same evening that Richard had sustained the wound, and the boy was a prisoner. He gave his name as Peter Basile, and he said he'd fired at Richard in revenge for our men killing both his father and his two brothers. He defied Richard to put him to death, but Richard — seemingly out of respect for the boy's bravery, or simply because he was ever the chivalrous fool — gave orders that the boy be freed and awarded a hundred shillings.'

'So the boy earned a bounty by killing the most powerful and respected monarch in Christendom?'

'He most certainly did not,' Mercadier replied with a malicious chuckle. 'After Richard's funeral I had him flayed alive, then hung.'

Hugh let that sink in before enquiring, 'So who will now rule England?'

Mercadier shrugged. 'A weighty question. It seems that prior to embarking upon his Crusade, Richard named young Arthur of Brittany as his heir, then took the precaution of marrying his mother to Ranulf of Chester. Since then Ranulf has deserted her, seemingly because of her nagging ways, but more importantly Richard is claimed by many to have forgiven his brother John to such an extent that he let it be known that he is to inherit. It is John who now accuses you of desertion, and commands that you be held in London pending his return for his coronation.'

'So has John been accepted by those magnates in a position to secure his accession?'

'Certainly those in England and Normandy, in the main. But there is still a faction in Anjou, Maine, and obviously Brittany, who insist that under their law the crown falls to Arthur. And by way of revenge against John for his recent change of allegiance, Philip of France has declared for Arthur.'

Hugh sighed heavily. 'We are destined for more warfare, it would seem.'

'You judge aright,' Mercadier confirmed, 'but therein lies your road to redemption.'

'Your meaning?'

Mercadier put down his wine mug and stared intently into Hugh's eyes. 'John's order was that you be taken up like a common criminal and thrown into the Tower dungeons to await his decision on the mode of your death. In that regard, he is as dangerous as his late father when angered. But it was I, along with your feudal overlord Ranulf of Chester, who persuaded him that he needed the ongoing loyalty of every proven warrior who could be summoned to his battle banner. We are destined to clash arms with Philip of France again, and John may be persuaded to spare your life if you pledge support for his cause.'

'Even though he accounts me a deserter?'

'You deserted King Richard, did you not? John regards himself as a new broom to sweep the stable, and would be prepared to wipe clean the slate of your misdeeds if you sign up for service in his train.'

'As you describe matters, I have little choice,' Hugh sighed. 'I had hoped to put the battlefields behind me, and simply play the lord of the manor while watching my son progress towards manhood.'

'And so you must!' Edwina challenged him as she reappeared in the manor house doorway, leading Geoffrey by the hand. 'You have a wife and child to consider, and yours is the head that governs the Earldom of Flint.'

'A head that will grace the ground in London if I don't take this opportunity to swear allegiance to our new king,' he told her. 'If you had listened to the whole of our conversation, you would know that Mercadier here has done me the greatest favour by intervening on my behalf with Prince John, who will shortly become King John, whose service I deserted. Now I have to answer for that, and preserve my head by re-entering the royal service.'

'Where your head will risk being lost in battle!' Edwina protested. 'Either way I seem fated to become a widow, and Geoffrey will grow up not knowing a father.'

'I now have more than my own head to preserve,' Hugh pointed out as he gestured towards Mercadier. 'This brave man, and good friend, has pledged his word to bring me before the new King in London. Should I not appear with him, it will be his head that is forfeit.'

Edwina appeared to have no answer to this, but as she turned to go back into the house, she urged, 'Leave before daybreak on the morrow, if you must go, for I could not bear a lengthy wait for your departure. I shall spend tonight in another chamber, perhaps with Nan — she was never known to desert me.'

With that she flounced back indoors, leaving Hugh speechless and Mercadier embarrassed as he quietly observed, 'That might be the wisest policy, my friend.'

The following morning the sun was just beginning to rise over the distant spires of Chester as Hugh tightened his mount's saddle leathers, and turned for one last look at the manor house. As he did so, the front entrance filled with Edwina's scurrying figure. She wore a long gown, with a cloak thrown over it to combat the early morning chill. She hastened towards him, eyes red from a night of tears, and flung herself at him in a passionate embrace.

'Take care not to leave a widow and *two* offspring to mourn your needless passing,' she whispered. 'I'm with child again.'

Hugh smiled at one familiar face after another as he stood to one side of the Tower armoury door, awaiting his turn to have his sword sharpened. These were all men that he'd served with in the days when he'd been helping King Richard regain his territories across the Channel. He wondered how many of them remembered that he'd once ordered their battle formations and examined their weaponry before leading a charge. To judge by the friendly smiles he was receiving in return, many of them did.

'Since when did you need to wait in line to have your weapon sharpened?' came a friendly voice, and Hugh turned to his feudal overlord, Ranulf of Chester, accompanied as ever by two of the largest men in his entourage as a personal bodyguard.

'These are all your men, as I recall.' Hugh nodded towards the steady coming and going through the armoury door.

'They are now yours, if you will undertake the commission,' Ranulf said, and suddenly it all made sense in Hugh's head. The moderately paced journey south to London, the comfortable inns along the way in which their reckoning had been paid by Mercadier with coin issued to him for the purpose, the comfortable billet in the garrison block at the Tower, and now the arrival of Ranulf.

'Do I have you to thank for the fact that I am not already in irons?' Hugh asked.

Ranulf nodded. 'Myself and Mercadier, who managed to persuade our new king that you did not desert out of cowardice, but that in fact you are one of the bravest men available to us — also one of the most skilled in warfare and battle tactics. Why *did* you desert, by the way?'

Hugh had already prepared his answer for the king and his interrogators, and this would be a good opportunity to rehearse it.

'The death of my father, a loyal servant of the Crown, and the need to resolve my affairs in Flint, as well as ensuring that my brother inherited the Repton estate, as King Richard had ordained. It was safe enough to leave the ranks at that time anyway, since we seemed to be gaining the upper hand over the French.'

'And now?'

'And now I am returned. It is true that I had little choice in the matter, but now that I am back in familiar surroundings I realise that a part of me will always crave martial action.'

'And how about ceremonial duties?' Ranulf asked. When Hugh looked back enquiringly, Ranulf waved an arm to indicate the square of men forming up in the centre of the parade ground. 'Prince John has honoured me with the duty of providing the armed escort when he progresses from his Palace of Westminster to the nearby abbey for his coronation as King of England. I wish you to lead them, as my bondsman and my Captain of the Royal Guard for the occasion. It is to be hoped that when His Majesty conveys his official thanks to his guard of honour following the ceremony, as is the custom, he will realise his mistake in adjudging you a traitor and a coward.'

'I doubt he will even recognise me,' Hugh objected.

Ranulf tapped his nose and grinned. 'You may leave it to me to ensure that he does.'

Three days later, Hugh gave the loyal salute as John emerged from the main doors of Westminster Palace and began the ceremonial walk of several hundred yards to the West Door of Westminster Abbey, where Archbishop of Canterbury Hubert Walter and the cream of England's nobility awaited their new monarch. John appeared not to recognise Hugh as he led the sixteen-man party, armed ceremonially with halberds, and more effectively with swords hanging from their belts, to the West Door. They turned and bowed John through the door.

Two hours later he was waiting in the Audience Chamber back at the palace, watching John being divested of his coronation robes and receiving the honeyed congratulations of magnate after magnate. Among them was Ranulf of Chester, who drew John to one side and led him to where Hugh was standing smartly to attention. He bowed obsequiously as Ranulf introduced him.

'The Captain of your Coronation Guard, sire. Earl Hugh of Flint.'

John's eyes narrowed. 'The deserter?'

'No deserter, sire,' Ranulf replied before Hugh could respond. 'The bravest fighting man I have ever encountered, and the obvious choice to lead your personal guard into the abbey.'

'Tomorrow at ten of the forenoon, here,' John snarled at Hugh as he pointedly turned his back on him and moved to the next man to be presented.

The following morning Hugh was standing nervously inside the Audience Chamber, an hour earlier than the time for which he had been summoned. Walter de Coutances, the ageing Archbishop of Rouen, came through the door that led from the Withdrawing Chamber and walked over to shake his hand.

'Welcome back into the royal service, Hugh. I was saddened to hear of the death of your father, who served England valiantly in the dark days that are hopefully now behind us. But in so doing he earned the ire of our new king, and I hear that also you have fallen into disfavour.'

Hugh nodded. 'I was meant to lead John's forces when he and King Richard were striving to regain control of Normandy. Then my father died just as we were gaining the upper hand, and I was granted leave to return to both his former estate in Repton, and my new estate in Flint. Regrettably I stayed overlong, but it would seem that my services were never required and that we now have total control of the royal lands across the Channel.'

'For the time being, certainly,' Walter nodded as he looked briefly behind him before continuing, 'but I am here at this early hour, out of respect for the memory of your father, to advise you of how matters currently stand, so that you may best organise your defence when you answer to our new king.'

'What must I learn?' Hugh asked, and de Coutances lowered his voice even further.

'John is not the only claimant to the legacy of the great King Richard. There is a royal nephew, Arthur of Brittany, who has the support of not only Philip of France but also the barons of Anjou, Maine and Touraine. They are led by the powerful and influential William des Roches, appointed by Arthur as Seneschal of Anjou. John retains Normandy, and was anointed as its duke some weeks ago, under my hand at Rouen. Prior to that he had attempted to take Le Mans from those forces of Arthur's that had besieged it, but was forced to retreat when Philip of France approached from the south with superior forces. In gratitude Arthur swore allegiance to Philip for all his estates, and John is now anxious to regroup and re-take Le Mans, preferably with his irksome nephew still inside it.'

'So he would be likely to spare this fighting man?' Hugh asked eagerly.

De Coutances shrugged. 'It is to be hoped that this will be the case, but regrettably John has proved himself time and again to be a man whose loyalties swing like an inn sign in a strong wind. He is as untrusting as was his father, and is cursed also with his vile temper. He lurches from periods of wild activity into pits of inertia, and in these latter moods it is almost impossible to move him to take such actions as are necessary, even for his own good. I also fear that he spurns to be guided by God.'

Hugh grimaced. 'Father would tell tales of King Henry's occasional blasphemy, and I seemingly had an uncle who died alongside the martyr Becket.'

De Coutances nodded sadly. '*Qualis pater, talis filius,*' he murmured. 'Like father, like son. That was sadly demonstrated even during his investiture as Duke of Normandy, when he scandalised all present by giggling and jostling with the young men in his immediate retinue while I was endeavouring to conduct the Mass. At one point he succeeded in dropping his ducal lance of office while overcome with hilarity. It was taken by many present as a bad omen for the future of the duchy. I am also advised that his whoring has become legendary, and it is said that he and Queen Isabella have not lain together for many months. This is despite the urgings of many, including myself; if he were to get a legitimate heir by her, then his cause would be all the more appealing to those who currently lean towards Arthur, but who might be persuaded otherwise by the prospect of a continuation of the dynasty.'

'It was surely the embarrassment of sons that led to the upheavals of recent years?' Hugh suggested.

'That is always John's argument. "I was the last in the line of heirs, and was always in the shadow of older brothers," he is wont to complain. "I would not wish that curse upon any son of mine." But clearly there is no current prospect of *any* heir, and Walter of Canterbury advises me that His Majesty has of late enquired as to the possibility of annulling his marriage to the queen on the grounds of their consanguinity. They are cousins of a sort, apparently.'

Just then the doors to the Withdrawing Chamber were thrown open by two pages, and into the Audience Chamber walked King John, accompanied by Ranulf of Chester and Mercadier. Hugh bowed the knee and kept his head down as he heard the group approaching and waited for the command to rise. When it didn't come he ventured to look upwards, and was relieved to note that John's attendants were both smiling. However, John's face remained stern.

'You may thank your two good friends here that you are not about to be taken out and hanged,' he announced. 'At least, not this time, but if you desert my service once more, that will be your fate. We are *ad idem* on that point, are we?'

'Yes, sire,' Hugh mumbled in what he hoped was a sufficiently humble tone. 'I shall henceforth serve you with unswerving loyalty wherever you may command.'

'You are familiar with Le Mans, in Normandy?'

'Indeed, sire.'

'And what of its defences?'

'As I recall, sire, its main defence is an ancient wall that is much in need of repair. It has no castle as such, but a cathedral that can be defended, as it once was by me when escorting the former Queen Berengaria and her entourage. But from the vantage point of an army laying siege to it, it presents a soft target.'

'It is to be hoped that your memory serves you well,' John replied coldly, 'since you may once again prove both your valour and your honour by laying siege to it and bringing my nephew Arthur to me, bound hand and foot. That is all.'

As he swept from the chamber, hastily followed by Ranulf, Mercadier hung back.

'You have faced more daunting tasks, I suspect?'

'I have indeed,' Hugh replied as he breathed more freely. 'Will you be joining me in the attack on Le Mans?'

'No,' Mercadier replied. 'I have the gentler task of escorting Queen Dowager Eleanor back to her former home in Poitiers, and thence on to Aquitaine; while you are busy in the north, I shall be securing the back door to the south. Ranulf will be by your side, I understand.'

'And King John?'

'He seemingly has business in Flanders and Boulogne, where he hopes to form further alliances. But no doubt he will be there to claim the glory when you smoke out his nephew. Do not fail him, is all I ask. My neck is as vulnerable as yours in these uncertain times, remember.'

# IV

Hugh looked across the flat plain towards the crumbling walls of Le Mans, behind which sat not only its magnificent cathedral but also what was left of a fading former mansion that was dignified by some as a castle. They were hidden inside a dense wood, a thousand of them under the notional command of Ranulf of Chester but in practice led by Hugh. They had been back across the Channel for over a month, and were awaiting news from further east, where John was seeking alliances with a view to bolstering his defence of Normandy.

'The men are returning, sir,' called a lookout from a tall poplar tree several hundred yards ahead.

'Send them direct to me,' Hugh called back.

The two forward scouts, dressed as farmers and equipped with a cart full of turnips that had been stolen from a farm half a day's ride to the west, had been sent into the town to reconnoitre and report back, and they did so in tones of bewilderment.

'There's no sign of any army in there, sir, and no flags flyin' from the château to suggest that anyone important's livin' there, least of all the French King or the Duke o' Brittany. The place is wide open to us if we strike now.'

'Did you speak to anyone while you were there?' Hugh asked.

The other scout nodded. 'I stopped at an alehouse and pretended that I was a travellin' cook from Rennes who was 'opin' to enter the service of Duke Arthur of Brittany, an' 'ad bin told that he was to be found here.'

'And what reply did you receive?'

'That 'e'd bin there some weeks ago, and that some of his men 'ad been billeted at the inn. Then they'd bin told to move out an' 'ead for Tours, where they were to meet with the King o' France. They left without payin', the man complained.'

'And how long ago was this?' Hugh asked.

The man shrugged. 'He didn't say — mainly 'cos I forgot to ask.'

Thanking the man for his report, Hugh returned to the clearing further back in the trees where he'd left Ranulf and his personal entourage.

'It seems that Arthur has headed further south, to meet Philip of France in Tours. What do you wish done now?'

Ranulf's face reflected his uncertainty. 'Our orders were to take the town, but that was in the belief that Arthur was there, since we were also ordered to take him. Do we stay in order to secure Le Mans, or do we skirt the town and head for Tours?'

'And face the full might of the entire French army?' Hugh asked sarcastically. 'We should perhaps wait for the king to join us. When do you expect him?'

Another shrug from Ranulf. 'It's difficult to say, since clearly it will depend upon what success he has met with in Flanders and Boulogne. Perhaps we should occupy the town and make it ready for his arrival, ensuring some comfort for him and welcome billets for our men.'

Hugh thought for a moment, then shook his head. 'If we reveal our presence, there are bound to be messages sent ahead to warn Arthur and his French allies that we are in pursuit of them. My preference is to skirt the town well to the west and go by way of Angers towards Tours. Angers is back in our possession, thanks to Mercadier, and has been since before the coronation. But perhaps we should await King John ere we move south.'

They were confined within the wood for a week, forced to forage for supplies from local farmlands, pulling crops from the ground and slaughtering cattle as their owners stood by helplessly. The fighting men grew more and more fractious as they were obliged to bed down nightly in forest undergrowth and leaf litter. Finally, the sound of distant battle horns drew their eyes to the east, where a large body of men was heading towards what had been meant as a temporary hideout, although there could be few within a fifty-mile radius who were not now aware that a large horde was encamped in the woods to the north of Le Mans.

For a few heart-stopping moments, it was believed that the force moving towards them might be the French advancing south to join with Arthur's forces; then Ranulf recognised the battle banners of Flanders and Boulogne. 'It would seem that His Majesty succeeded in gaining the alliance of the two most powerful lords north of Normandy,' he told Hugh.

An hour later John trotted his horse up to the sagging canvas that constituted the English command centre, accompanied by Baldwin IX of Flanders to his left, and Renaud of Boulogne on his other side. He dismounted and strode swiftly towards Ranulf. 'Why are you not holding Le Mans and the traitorous dog Arthur?' he demanded.

'He fled in the face of our advance, sire. Our best intelligence is that he was headed to Tours, there to liaise with Philip of France.'

'Dolts! Idiots!' John screamed as he stamped his spurred boot deep into the soft forest mulch. 'If the two forces meet up, they could cut Normandy in two along the Loire Valley! Why did you not pursue them when you could?'

'Our orders were to take Le Mans, sire,' Ranulf reminded him as the colour left his face.

'Then why are you sitting here like lusty milkmaids in the middle of a forest, awaiting your ploughman amour? You!' he yelled across at Hugh. 'Have you forgotten how to lay siege to a place?'

'No, sire,' Hugh replied through gritted teeth. 'It can be taken at any time, but we chose not to disclose our presence here, in case word was carried south to Arthur in Tours.'

'You have been here for several weeks,' John said, red-faced. 'No doubt you have been living off the surrounding land, and your presence here will now be known to every cow, sheep, squirrel and rabbit for miles around. I shall show you how to take a town that has played host to your enemy, and I shall do so without your assistance. Now give me wine, or have you forgotten how to entertain a king as well?'

An hour later, slightly drunk, John broke the cover of the wood and rode into Le Mans with the combined forces of Flanders and Boulogne that he had brought with him. Within minutes the screams could be heard even from the wood, and before long the tell-tale smoke plumes revealed that the wooden structures within the town had been put to the torch. It was not long before the stragglers from the party that John had taken into Le Mans returned with white faces, some shaking with fear, as they recounted the slaughter that John had inflicted on innocent townspeople, including children. The butchered corpses had been left lying in the streets as a warning of what to expect if they ever again played host to an enemy of England.

Hugh shook his head in disbelief as the men were brought to their tent to report the day's events, and Ranulf sat open-mouthed.

'Was there any need for such slaughter?' he asked.

Hugh spat into the earth. 'None whatsoever,' he hissed. 'He's made a permanent enemy of a strategic town, and has demonstrated to his recently acquired allies that he is a madman who lacks military wisdom. He has also, to me at least, demonstrated the most obvious trait of any bully, namely his cowardice. God alone knows what he will order us to do next.'

'What would *you* do, given a free choice?' Ranulf asked.

After a moment's thought, Hugh nodded back towards Le Mans. 'I would have held that town in conditions of friendship, using it as a base to keep Arthur from meeting up with Philip of France. Then I would have headed south, to silence Arthur's threat, and take him prisoner, in the belief that Philip would then retreat north back to Paris. As matters stand, we have wrecked the most obvious base for preventing the two forces from joining up, and left a foul taste in the mouths of innocent Normans regarding England and its new king.'

John returned several hours later, with several of the town's leading officials being dragged behind the horses of his immediate followers, stumbling on tired legs. 'These should fetch a pretty penny!' he yelled at Hugh and Ranulf as he rode past them. 'Now bring wine and meet me where my battle headquarters have been established to the south of this forest bolthole of yours.'

Night was falling as Hugh finally managed to persuade John to send out scouts to the north and south, to learn if the might of France had been added to Arthur's claim to the throne of England. Within three more days, they had learned that while John had been inflicting his cruelty on an innocent town that would forever remember him as the Devil incarnate, Arthur had skirted Tours and met with Philip well to the south of them, at Blois, and they were now headed back to Paris together. John had thrown away a valuable opportunity to prevent what threatened to be a very powerful alliance.

If John was aware of his folly, he gave no sign of it as he ordered everyone north, back to the safety of Caen, from where he sent for the bishops of Lisieux, Bayeux and Avranches. It was hardly likely to be the case that he required spiritual guidance, and even less likely that he sought to confess his sins. There was therefore wild speculation as to why he had summoned three bishops, rather than call for Walter de Coutances to cross back over from England. Then came the astonishing news.

'John has prevailed upon the bishops to annul his marriage to Queen Isabella!' Ranulf announced as he slid onto the bench beside Hugh to help himself to a breakfast of ham and cheese. 'What is he about, think you?'

Hugh gave a gentle snort. 'Why do you seek rational explanations for the actions of a man who has quite clearly taken leave of his wits?' he asked. 'The next thing we know he'll be betrothed to his horse.'

'We are bound in his service, whether he be witless or not,' Ranulf reminded him. 'And it is rumoured that Arthur of Brittany is now safely installed in the French Court in Paris, being tutored alongside the young heir Louis, since they are of similar ages. Will we be ordered to sack Paris next, think you?'

'God forbid,' Hugh muttered, 'although it would not surprise me to learn that we are bound there for a peace treaty. Mercadier has returned from Poitiers, where he has been escorting Eleanor on a tour of her southern lands. Seemingly she has paid homage to Philip for Poitou and Aquitaine, to prevent Philip ceding them to Arthur, and she plans in turn to declare John as her heir. If that be the case, then our lord and master will need to travel to Paris to have his inheritance confirmed by his notional overlord.'

Ranulf chuckled. 'So John will be required to bow the knee to Philip? I can just visualise the look on his face when he does so.'

'I told you so,' Hugh said to Ranulf out of the corner of his mouth as they left the Audience Chamber later that morning, each with their separate instructions. Hugh was to remain in Caen with the main body of John's forces, and take what steps he could to prevent the desertion of any more men from Flanders and Boulogne. Ranulf, for his part, was to accompany John south to Paris, where he hoped to convert the current stalemate into a truce that would give him time to venture south-west to Poitiers and Aquitaine, for reasons that he declined to disclose.

Once John had departed, accompanied by Ranulf and some of his best captains, Hugh set about forming a combined force out of the shambolic remains of his own men, the best of whom had gone to Paris with John, and what was left of the retinues of Baldwin of Flanders and Renaud of Boulogne, both of whom had returned home in disgust after John's actions in Le Mans. More than once Hugh was tempted to make a sea crossing back to his estate in Flint, where Edwina would soon be nearing her lying in time with their new addition, but on each occasion he reminded himself that John was both unstable and unforgiving. By deserting his service again, even for a brief time, he would be risking not only his own life and estate, but also the lives of a pregnant Edwina and an innocent boy of seven.

A month later Ranulf returned, and the expression on his face said it all. He lost no time in being admitted to Hugh's chambers, and after accepting a mug of wine with a hand that was trembling, but seemingly from rage rather than fear, he passed on the almost unbelievable tidings.

'He would not be advised or counselled by me, but simply blundered into the worst peace treaty I have ever heard of. Why take me as his alleged expert in diplomacy when he insisted on making all the decisions — every one of them fatal to our interests?'

Fearful that Ranulf was about to expire from apoplexy, Hugh bade him take deep breaths, then take his time disclosing the details of what had reduced him to quivering disbelief. Then he felt his own blood running cold as he learned the details of the Treaty of Le Goulet, named after the island where it had been signed, which lay in the middle of the Seine near Vernon, to the north-east of Paris and within the Vexin.

John had clearly focused on two issues, to the detriment of all others, and had made concessions that in the long term could prove disastrous for England. First was his desire to be acknowledged as King of England, and second was the need to remove his nephew Arthur from under the protection of France. This was achieved by the single expedient of John recognising Philip as the suzerain of the entire Angevin empire as it had been at its height during the reign of John's father Henry, in return for which Philip withdrew his support for Arthur's claim as Richard's heir.

In the process, John had abandoned his most recent allies in Flanders and Boulogne by acknowledging that they were vassals of France. Needless to say, he had made that concession without consulting them, and had added salt to those wounds by pledging not to support any rebellions by either of them once the news leaked out.

The fact that one could never rely on John's assurance of friendship was further underlined by John's abandonment of the Vexin to French control. It lay between Normandy and the Île-de-France ruled over by Philip, and had in previous years been a valuable buffer between the two nations, and a respected outpost of English interests. Now it had been handed back to France without a whimper or a protest. While the de Montfort family that had estates in Évreux would no longer have divided loyalties, given that their other estate of Montfort-l'Amaury lay within the Île-de-France, Ranulf was personally incensed by this capitulation, since Évreux had been his mother's birthplace.

But there was even more evidence that John would make a finer bullock cart driver than a diplomat. Given that Anjou and Brittany were already within the Angevin lands of which John had already been recognised as the ruler, albeit under the suzerainty of France, there had been no need for the further payment of twenty thousand marks that Philip demanded by way of relief for John's acquisition of the title. Finally, since John already held Aquitaine as heir to his mother Eleanor, there had been no need to secure it by way of a marriage treaty that would annexe it to French interests, but John had agreed to arrange for Philip's heir, the young Louis, to be pledged in marriage to John's niece Blanche of Castile, daughter of his sister Leonora. In due course this would drop the strategically valuable, and hitherto independent, kingdom across the Pyrenees into French control on the death of its current ruler, King Alfonso.

'He's the laughing stock of Europe!' Ranulf groaned. 'He was negotiating from such a position of power, with the full might of his father's vast inheritance behind him, yet he bargained as if he was a prisoner begging for his life. He could simply have defied Philip, who is rumoured to be in bad odour with the Pope on account of his marital misdeeds, and is anxious to put warfare behind him. Instead John yielded ultimate sovereignty to him, and in exchange for what? A few years of peace that he was likely to be able to enjoy anyway? Little wonder that his own soldiers — at least, those who accompanied me — have taken to calling him "John Softsword"!'

The following day also brought new instructions for Mercadier, summoned by John from Poitiers, where he had been tasked with the daily protection of Eleanor and her estates both in that region and in her native Aquitaine. Mercadier was at a loss to understand why he had been summoned, and was apprehensive that he had in some way caused John some displeasure. His fears were quickly laid to rest when advised that he was to carry secret despatches back to the royal mother with instructions to travel across the Pyrenees into Castile and prepare her granddaughter Blanche for marriage to the young Louis of France. 'I do not trust anyone else with the task,' John told him, 'and I myself must return to England in order to secure her dowry. It is a large sum, and I shall require a stronger than usual escort — who would you recommend? Young Chester does not possess the stomach for fighting.'

'What of his able second in command, Hugh of Flint?' Mercadier suggested. 'He is a doughty fighting man, and might well relish the prospect of returning to England, where his wife is due to deliver their second child.'

'Can he be trusted?' John asked suspiciously. 'I have found him to be arrogant and difficult to dissuade when he believes himself to be in the right.'

'That is because invariably he *is* right, in my experience,' Mercadier said. 'And since you have graciously entrusted me with the more important mission of the two, who better to undertake the simple matter of guarding a large sum of money? There can be few aspects of that duty with which he could disagree.'

# V

Two months later Hugh rode into the courtyard of his Flint estate with trepidation. It was common for women — even healthy ones like Edwina — to die in childbirth. After securing a grudging two-week leave of absence from John, he'd spent his four-day ride from London veering between anticipating the joy of holding Edwina and their newborn in his arms, and envisioning the horror of being advised that his wife had died while calling for him.

Hugh dismounted and turned, and there stood Nan, peering with aged eyes. She walked slowly towards him and his heart lurched dangerously under his leather riding tunic.

'It's me, Nan — how fares your mistress?'

'Well enough, for all the attention you bestowed upon her when she was in the throes of childbirth.'

'She is well? I mean, she survived?'

Nan tutted in exasperation. 'Of *course* she survived, you impudent young... Oh, I mean... Please forgive me, Master, but I was overcome with rage at the mere suggestion. I've delivered more infants than I can remember, and although some of those were claimed by God, I've never yet lost a mother.'

'God be praised! And thank you, Nan.'

'Is that *all* you wish to ask of me?' she replied testily. 'Do you not wish to know if it is a boy or a girl?'

'Yes, of course, but my first concern was for your mistress, and my wife.'

'That's as it should be, and I can now tell you that you have a healthy baby girl. She was large for a girl, to my mind, and my lovely Edwina had a hard time of it, but all the better for the infant. She is feeding well, and has a good set of lungs. You'll find the countess in your upstairs chamber.'

Thanking Nan yet again, Hugh clomped eagerly up the narrow wooden staircase and burst into the bedchamber, only to be admonished sharply by a sleepy-looking Edwina as the infant murmured and whimpered in its cot by the window, threatening to wake again.

'I fed her only an hour or so ago,' Edwina complained, 'and you come blundering up here like a bullock that broke loose from a market stall! If she wakes, it will take forever to get her back to sleep.'

Hugh walked carefully to the bedside, took Edwina's hand in his, leaned down, and kissed her on the lips. 'Thank you for making me a father once again. Now, would you care to tell me how overjoyed you are at my safe return?'

'All in good time,' she replied with a warm smile. 'In the meantime, go and admire your daughter in that cot over there that was once mine. Then you can help me choose her name.'

'I thought perhaps "Edith",' Edwina suggested the following morning as they sat at breakfast. 'And you haven't come up with anything at all — what's occupying your mind?'

Hugh sighed. 'Sorry. "Edith" sounds nice, so let's call her that. Is it Welsh?'

'No, English, I think. Wasn't there once a queen with that name? And you haven't told me why you seem so distracted. You have to leave again, don't you?'

'Not just yet, but soon. The king allowed me two weeks, but eight days of those two weeks are taken up just riding up here and back.'

'I hope that you aren't about to suggest that I move down to London with the children — I've had quite enough of Court life, thank you.'

'It's how we met,' he reminded her.

'And that was about the only good thing that came from it. All that posturing and false manners, having to look one's best before breakfast, remembering not to break wind at table and so forth. I'm happy to stay here, unless I'm also ordered south by our new king. What's he like?'

'Arrogant, foul-tempered, incapable of making a sensible decision, vainglorious and mean — and believe me, those are his *good* points.'

'I don't suppose you can get out of serving him in the near future?'

'Only on the end of a rope, I imagine. He's such a fool that he requires men like me to save his neck from the last rash decision he made. That's when he can be bothered to make one at all — there are entire days when he angrily refuses to discuss important matters. He just sits around, drinks to excess and shouts at the servants.'

Edwina grimaced. 'It's difficult to believe that he's Richard's younger brother.'

'He has Richard's cruel side, anyway. But let's not spend all our time talking about him. How do you spend *your* time while I'm away?'

Edwina nodded to where Geoffrey was picking up pieces of cheese, sniffing them, then either licking them and putting them back on the serving dish or throwing them into the rushes. 'There's your answer. Making sure that our son doesn't come to any harm is a full-time duty — ask any mother.'

'So how will you manage a second?'

'That's what Nan's for,' she replied as she took his hand. 'I thought we might go fishing again today. While you were away I went down to our favourite spot almost every day, and somehow it made you feel closer. A few more happy memories will serve me well when you have to ride south again.'

That day came all too soon. With a sinking heart, Hugh handed his mount to a stable groom at Westminster and sought out Ranulf of Chester, who advised him with a long countenance that Mercadier was dead, and that he and Hugh were to prepare to travel without delay in John's entourage to Bordeaux.

'How did Mercadier die, and why Bordeaux?' he asked.

Ranulf shook his head sadly. 'The answer to both questions is the same. Queen Dowager Eleanor was travelling to Castile in order to bring her granddaughter back to Normandy for her wedding to Louis of France, but not far south of Poitiers she was ambushed by Hugh de Lusignan, who had taken up the claim of his forebears for the return of La Marche from the royal demesne. Mercadier had been delayed in Rouen by other business, and was therefore not by her side. Anyway, the outcome was that the king was obliged to concede the county to Hugh, despite the rival claim of Aymer of Angoulême, and Eleanor was allowed to cross the mountains and collect the bride.'

'And how did Mercadier come to die?' Hugh pressed him.

'On the way back, the royal party halted at Bordeaux. Mercadier unwisely took himself to a local inn, where he came across an old enemy and was hacked to death in a side street on his departure from there. Queen Eleanor is beside herself and refusing to move another foot outside her residence in Fontevrault. The intended bride Blanche is currently being held secure by the Archbishop of Bordeaux, and we are ordered to provide her with safe escort back into Normandy for the marriage ceremony.'

'It is not being held in Paris?' Hugh queried.

Ranulf shook his head. 'Pope Innocent has placed the whole of France under interdict because of King Philip's dalliance with his latest mistress, and John has offered to host the ceremony.'

'To my mind, he's far too anxious to appease the French in everything,' Hugh muttered.

Ranulf nodded in agreement. 'However, we must do as we are bidden, so don't get too comfortable in your quarters. We ride out again two days hence.'

The wedding ceremony went without a hitch just inside the boundaries of Normandy. Hugh and Ranulf were preparing for a return to Rouen when John announced that he had been invited to a banquet at Lusignan, a two-day ride south of Poitiers. This was partly to celebrate the accession to La Marche of Count Hugh, and partly to broker a possible peace between the houses of Lusignan and Angoulême, to its south, whose Count Aymer had previously laid claim to La Marche. John was anticipating a cold reception by his fellow guest, and was therefore insistent that he be accompanied by a suitable force of men in addition to his two regular escorts. Hugh and Ranulf sighed, but did as they were told, and rode either side of John as they arrived at Lusignan.

Present at the several banquets thrown in John's honour was the beautiful and precocious thirteen-year-old daughter of Aymer of Angoulême. Her name was Isabella, and she was already betrothed to Hugh of Lusignan, the brother of John's host, but John was instantly smitten. His immediate companions Hugh and Ranulf gazed on in stunned amazement as the man they knew only as a foul-mouthed, bad-tempered, merciless bully played the part of the cultured and attentive troubadour, dancing gently with the young beauty and never leaving her side even when they took a short break from the quadrilles and circle dances. For her part, the young Isabella seemed both delighted and somewhat taken aback to be so enthusiastically attended by a powerful king, while her father Aymer looked on with a thoughtful gaze, but did nothing to intervene.

'The man is bewitched,' Ranulf declared as they shared a frugal supper after one of the lengthiest and richest banquets either man could remember. 'I don't believe he cursed once, and I could not detect a single one of his defiant farts during the entire meal.'

'He is perhaps in love,' Hugh suggested as fond memories returned of his days in thrall to the dark beauty who he'd made his wife.

'But she's betrothed to Hugh de Lusignan,' Ranulf protested.

Hugh gave him a wry smile. 'Not for long, if His Majesty has set his mind on her,' he predicted. 'Watch for some process whereby de Lusignan is removed from the scene — perhaps even by assassination.'

In the event, de Lusignan's departure from his brother's Court was manipulated far less violently. He was sent to England on a mission for King John that amounted to little more than advising Chancellor Walter that the king would be delayed by affairs in Lusignan. Once he had departed, John was rumoured to be in closed discussions with Aymer of Angoulême, prior to his returning home with his protesting daughter in tow, outraged that the marriage that she had been preparing for would not now be taking place.

But her trousseau did not go to waste, nor was the date of her marriage put back by a single day. On the very day that she should have been wed to Hugh de Lusignan in Eu, she stood before the altar in Bordeaux Cathedral and became the somewhat confused, and more than slightly aggrieved, Queen of England at the hand of its archbishop. John had a new queen.

Initially there seemed to be no reaction from the jilted bridegroom, as the newlyweds journeyed under escort from Bordeaux, via Poitiers and Chinon, to Fontevrault, where the future queen met the former one, and they seemed to get on well together, given their common backgrounds in the south of the continent. Then it was back across the Channel following a triumphant progress through Normandy, and Isabella was crowned Queen of England by Archbishop Hubert Walter in Westminster Abbey. The new queen was beautiful, John was besotted with his young bride, and for a short while England rejoiced. Then the doubts began to creep in, and John overplayed his hand.

Hugh had succeeded in obtaining leave of absence while John proudly showed off his new bride around the nation. He rode enthusiastically back to Flint, only to be advised that his mother Adele had died, and that his brother Robert had dedicated a shrine to her inside the local Repton Priory, where he had received his education, and which had a suitable Chapel of Our Lady in which to lay her remains. Hugh took Edwina and their two children on a mournful journey south, and they knelt in prayer before the memorial plinth beneath which Adele's bones had been laid to rest. He then told young Geoffrey as much as he knew about the family's history, stretching back to the days when Saxon England had first been invaded by the dynasty that still ruled the nation, and a distant ancestor had been knighted for his services in ensuring that the two communities did not wipe each other out in an ongoing war of attrition.

They had barely been back in Flint for a week when a messenger arrived from the neighbouring estate of Chester, passing on to Hugh an urgent request that he ride to Lincoln for the funeral of the recently deceased Bishop Hugh. He kissed Edwina and each of the children, apologising profusely for his departure, and rode hard across the East Midlands, reaching Lincoln just as the bell of its mighty cathedral was tolling for Evening Mass.

He found Ranulf leaving with the royal party, and was advised that he'd missed the funeral by three days.

'Why was I needed so urgently, simply to mourn a dead bishop?' he asked with irritation.

Ranulf shook his head. 'Clearly not for that. But the king fears some sort of revolt as the result of his impetuous marriage.' He produced a parchment from under his jacket. 'If Hugh had not died when he did, he would probably have been hanged anyway, since His Majesty clearly has little regard for either the Church or those who control it. But he *does* have regard for his image throughout the nation, and on his deathbed — perhaps because he knew that he would then be beyond any possible royal wrath — the bishop is reported to have said as follows.' He then read from the document in hushed tones: '*The descendants of King Henry must bear the curse pronounced in Holy Scripture: The multiplied brood of the wicked shall not thrive; and bastard slips shall not take deep root nor any fast foundation.*' And again: '*The children of adulterers shall be rooted out. The present King of France will avenge the memory of his virtuous father, King Louis, upon the children of the faithless wife who left him to unite with his enemy. And as the ox eats down the grass to its very roots, so shall Philip of France entirely destroy this race.'*

Hugh grimaced. 'You would be well counselled not to be caught with that poison in your possession. The king has a high regard for his mother, as we both know, and that was a vicious condemnation of her hasty marriage to his father so shortly after the dissolution of her marriage to Philip's father. How has the king reacted?'

'He was like a forest fire,' Ranulf replied, 'and none dared approach him for two days. We were convinced that the bishop's corpse would be tied to a stake and burned, but in the end John was prevailed upon to allow a decent Christian burial to a cleric who many admired in his earlier years.'

'One wonders how King Philip will react, should he learn of the dire prediction that his will be the hand to smite the Angevin descendants,' Hugh observed quietly. 'Why did you need me here?'

'You are summoned to the Christmas Court at Guildford, where John wishes to be assured that we all love and fear him in equal measure, and receive the loyal Yuletide greetings due to his new queen.'

'Is that all?' Hugh demanded, annoyed. 'What of our *own* families, deprived of our presence on those most holy of days, when we celebrate Christ's birth?'

'John cares nothing for the Nativity, nor ought else to do with the Christian faith,' Ranulf whispered as he looked nervously over his shoulder. 'But to judge by the hours he keeps in the royal bedchamber with his child bride, he is mindful of creating a wholly different birth.'

Shortly after the Christmas Court had dispersed, John received a formal written protest from Hugh de Lusignan regarding the theft of his former fiancée, which John pointedly ignored. Further incensed, Hugh stirred various Poitevin barons into a rebellion, to which John reacted by confiscating La Marche and bestowing it upon his new father-in-law Count Aymer of Angoulême. He further underlined his point by sending men at arms to seize the Castle of Driencourt, a possession of Hugh's brother Ralph. He could hardly have been surprised — and it was doubtful whether or not he even cared — when the Lusignans revoked their allegiance to John and appealed to his feudal overlord Philip of France.

Their timing was not auspicious, since Philip was in negotiations with the wily and powerful Pope Innocent to lift the interdict under which France was labouring, and was not anxious to recommence warfare with England, which at that time was in good standing with Rome. In angry frustration, the Lusignans began pillaging and plundering all over Poitou, and Eleanor sent urgent despatches to John, requesting that he cross the Channel to suppress the uprising that might one day place even her retreat at Fontevrault at risk.

He lost no time in moving the entire Court to the recently constructed, and allegedly impregnable, icon of English military prowess, the fortress at Château Gaillard. It both overlooked and guarded the Seine Valley in the Vexin, and had been excluded from the concessions made by John during the Treaty of Le Goulet. Content to leave the pacification of Poitou in the hands of those barons who remained loyal to him, and to ignore the indignant and ongoing complaints of the Lusignans, John lavished his lustful attentions on his new wife, scandalising the more prurient of his courtiers, and alarming those, such as Hugh and Ranulf, who could see the danger of such myopic indolence, by lying in bed with her until dinner time each day.

Then came the first crack in the wall. Constance of Brittany died, and whatever influence she had hitherto enjoyed over her son Arthur was removed, leaving him to fall more and more under the influence of his surrogate father figure Philip of France and his all but adoptive brother, the young Louis. He was prevailed upon to align his cause with that of the Lusignans, who sent yet another protest to the French Court after Pope Innocent lifted his interdict. This time, Philip adjudged the moment appropriate to act upon them all.

In April of 1202 John was summoned by Philip to present himself to the French Court, and answer to his feudal overlord for the complaints regarding his behaviour that had been lodged by the Lusignans, for whom Philip was also the overlord. This was a legitimate request, and in accordance with feudal law and tradition, but John's arrogant response was that as King of England and Duke of Normandy he was not answerable to any feudal authority. Philip's equally terse reply was to the effect that John was being summoned in relation to his estates in Aquitaine, Poitou and Anjou, for which he had conceded fealty in the ill-advised Treaty of Le Goulet. When John also ignored the deadline for appearing in even that capacity, Philip declared that John had forfeited his titles to all but Normandy. He then launched his well-prepared attack on two fronts.

First of all he knighted the fifteen-year-old Arthur of Brittany, betrothed him to his daughter Marie, then accepted his homage as his newly created vassal of Anjou, Maine, Touraine and Poitou. He then gave him a small army of two hundred French knights with which to occupy his new estates, and while Arthur marched boldly towards Poitou, Philip led a huge force north out of Paris to enforce his authority in the Vexin.

Not only was John totally unprepared for this two-pronged attack on his possessions across the Channel, but he was anxious regarding the safety of his mother Eleanor in her retreat at Fontevrault. Arthur might be her grandson, but he had been held back for too long by the uncle she had always favoured, and was anxious to secure her as a hostage. For one thing, he was aware that the elderly matriarch of the Angevin dynasty was one of the few people for whose safety John might be prepared to bargain, and more to the point Arthur was supported by the still smarting Hugh de Lusignan. The plan was that Eleanor might be bartered for the handing over of Queen Isabella.

Hugh was hardly surprised to be summoned by John and ordered south, to provide a bodyguard for Eleanor, convey her to a place of safety outside Poitou, and preferably bring her to Château Gaillard.

'If you fail me in this, you will hang!' John threatened him. 'I will follow with a larger army, but to you I entrust the task of making a fast crossing into Anjou and Poitou, thereafter guarding my mother with your life in some secure fortress to which I may bring a relieving party.'

Hugh set off with fifty of his best armed men, and by exchanging horses at regular intervals, eating and drinking while still on horseback, and stopping only to stretch their aching limbs and answer calls of nature, they reached Fontevrault within the week. Hugh was welcomed warmly by Eleanor, who was genuinely overcome with grief when advised that Adele had been laid to rest in Repton Priory earlier that year. Then she enquired as to what was to happen next.

'Your son has given orders that you be conveyed from here further east, to a place of greater safety outside of Poitou, and if possible to his mighty fortress of Château Gaillard,' Hugh told her.

'Richard had that built, as you will recall, and it is said to be impregnable. But how long shall we be on the road? I doubt that I could ride a horse for the two weeks or so that the journey might take, even at the height of this warm summer that we've been enjoying.'

'If you are prepared to travel during all the daylight hours, borne in a litter, then it might be possible, Your Majesty,' Hugh replied as tactfully as he could. 'The further away from Poitou the better, so that even if we do not make the sanctuary of the château, you will still be saved. Your son is close behind me with a larger force, and the further east we travel, the greater the prospect of meeting up with him on his way south-west to meet you.'

'Time was that I could match any man on horseback,' Eleanor said nostalgically, 'but it shall be as you say. This will not be the first time that you have saved my life, will it? I still remember that awful shipwreck on the coast of Cyprus, and I forgot to ask after the health of that delightful Welsh girl that you married.'

'She is now the mother of two beautiful children,' he replied. 'A boy of eight and a girl just over a year old. But let us lose no time in organising your flight, along with perhaps only one or two ladies in attendance, since they will only slow us down.'

'I can assure you that *this* lady will not,' she said. 'And thank God that for once John has demonstrated sound judgment in his choice of men.'

Their immediate plans were cast into disarray when word reached them from scouts whom Hugh had left on the road north that Arthur had joined forces with Hugh de Lusignan and was already in Tours, several days' ride to their north-east. If they continued north, as they had planned, hoping to reach safety across the Normandy border in Le Mans, they could be intercepted by Arthur's forces.

'We must perhaps move further south,' Hugh suggested, 'so that when Arthur and his supporters pursue us — as undoubtedly they will — they may be overrun from the north by the king and his greater army. Arthur is reckoned to have less than five hundred men, whereas your son can muster two thousand or more — perhaps even more than that as he progresses through Normandy. What we need is a safe haven further south of here, but still within Poitou.'

'Mirebeau,' Eleanor suggested. 'The town is old, but its castle may be defended until John arrives to lift any siege. Let us waste no further time!'

Four days later they were installed behind the ancient walls of the castle at Mirebeau, whose crumbling stonework promised little in the way of protection should a force of any size lay siege to it. They had barely settled in when their forward scouts gave warning of a moderately large body of armed men riding across country from Châtellerault, and Hugh made the strategic decision not to waste men and resources on defending the town by which they were surrounded, but to risk everything on a last-ditch defence of the castle.

He was gazing down forlornly at the knots of enemy knights who seemed to occupy every street of the town, whose gates they had sealed behind them, with only one left open for the delivery of supplies, when a message was brought to him by a guard on the postern gate: 'Duke Arthur wishes to enter in peace to parley with his beloved grandmother.'

When hastily consulted, and despite Hugh's better judgment, Eleanor readily agreed to have him admitted. When Hugh tried yet again to dissuade her, she raised a hand to silence him. 'If nothing else, it will buy us some time before John can come to our relief,' she said. 'And Arthur *is* family, after all.'

Hugh bit back the words he would like to have uttered regarding the family values of the Angevin brood, and gave an order that Arthur be admitted.

# VI

Arthur hardly looked like a rival for John's crown as he entered the Hall of Mirebeau Castle, walked the length of the chamber, knelt before his grandmother and took the proffered hand in order to kiss it. He was tall for his fifteen years, but it was as if he'd put all his efforts into his height, because he was reedy of body, and over-long in the arms and legs. Hugh was put in mind of a scarecrow in the fertile fields of Repton, and the cuirass covering Arthur's leather jerkin did nothing to give him any military bearing. Instead, he seemed almost penitent as he looked up into Eleanor's face and listened to her admonition, an old lady chastising an errant grandson.

'What means this treachery, Arthur?' she demanded. 'You are a disgrace to your father's memory, laying siege to your own ancestor and violating your oath of fealty to your overlord. What have you to say for yourself?'

'That I regret the need for the actions of my men, but that they are justified by the dishonour and betrayal of another of your sons. My Uncle John has stolen lands that belong to my own liege lord Philip of France, and has made off with the bride intended for another vassal of the same lord. He scorns to appear before the Court of France to answer for his actions, and I come as the ambassador of that Court to insist that he do so.'

'Laying siege to your own grandmother in the process? The woman who bore the son who made you his heir?' Eleanor demanded, playing for time and hoping to negotiate a peaceful truce that would endure until John arrived with his main force.

Arthur's face set in what might almost have been a smile. 'Were my Uncle Richard still in life, this would not be happening. As it is, out of respect for your person, I am offering you safe conduct from here. My men have the town firmly within their possession and there is but one way out, which would require you and your escort to ride right through them. I pledge my soul that if you and your immediate entourage leave peacefully, you will be allowed to return unharmed to your refuge in Fontevrault.'

Hugh looked anxiously across at Eleanor from where he was standing a few feet to her right, and could almost feel the quivering of her bony frame as she fixed Arthur with a glare that would drop a hawk from the sky.

'You may be Geoffrey's son, but you have inherited Richard's foolhardy bravery and John's haughty arrogance,' she replied in a voice edged with steel. 'You have the temerity, as my vassal for your Poitevin estates — along with peasants who are my liegemen and who all owe fealty to me, and me alone — to offer *me* safe passage out of my *own* castle! Furthermore, you lay siege to your own elderly grandmother and impliedly threaten her, with men at arms, that if she does not vacate her own demesne she will come to harm. Fie on you, ungrateful brat that you are! Take your unworthy person from my sight before I have you thrown out or — should you persist in remaining one moment longer — I may choose to have you hung from my walls. Out — *now*!'

Arthur bowed, turned and walked steadily back through the Hall. As he reached the door, he turned and bade her farewell. 'I do not think that we shall meet again in this life.'

Once the door had closed behind him, Eleanor seemed to crumple where she sat, and Hugh walked swiftly to her side, fearing that she might have had a seizure. Instead, she looked up at him through tear-filled eyes and asked, 'Was I too harsh? After all, he is my own flesh and blood.'

'If anything, Your Majesty, you were too mild,' Hugh replied with a sigh of relief. 'But it is to be hoped that King John arrives without further delay.'

John and his initial army had in fact been undergoing a forced march ever since leaving Chinon, covering the eighty-three miles in two days. On the way he had been joined by William des Roches, Seneschal of Anjou, who offered to join his men to the royal party in return for John's word that he would not execute any of the rebels once they retook Mirebeau, and that Arthur would be unharmed, albeit held secure. On that understanding the royal forces moved quickly to Mirebeau, and the main body of mounted knights, led by the Lord of Brecon, William de Braose, made hasty use of the town gate that had been left open for the delivery of supplies to Arthur's besieging force.

The first that Hugh knew of the arrival of the relief force was when he was awoken from a deep slumber by a page who advised him that there was fighting in the streets. He hastily donned his leather jerkin and thick hose, but prior to struggling into his battle armour he looked out of the window at the scene of wholesale slaughter revealed by the rising sun.

Arthur, along with Hugh de Lusignan and their immediate seconds in command, had been at breakfast, and John's vanguard, led by the battle-hardened William de Braose, had waited in the surrounding undergrowth until they saw guards being changed on the only gate to the town that remained open. This was always a moment of weakness in a force's defences, when eyes were looking inwards, rather than staring outwards for the approach of potential enemies. The gate guards now lay with slit throats, and John's largely mercenary force was pillaging at will through the township, stepping over the writhing corpses of those they had surprised and overwhelmed. It was a gruesome and merciless sight, but Hugh heaved deep sighs of relief when he spotted Ranulf among those taking prisoners, and hurried down to the queen dowager's suite of rooms with the glad tidings that John had finally lifted the siege, and that she was free to return to Fontevrault. 'But,' he added, 'if you would be advised by me, it might be best not to venture onto the streets until they have been cleared of the evidence of our release.'

When he returned to his chambers, he was advised that he had a visitor. The man was dressed as if for battle, and there were smears of blood streaking his face. But he looked friendly enough as he walked towards Hugh with an outstretched hand.

'We have not met before, yet we are neighbours when we are both back in Wales. I am William de Braose, Lord of Brecon and the infeft lord of many other Welsh Marcher estates, the closest to yours being in Radnor. I am here this day with a request for your assistance.'

Hugh gave a grimace in response. 'From what I have seen of the slaughter in the streets, some of which you have brought indoors on your face, you do not require any assistance from me.'

'The slaughter was largely at the urging of des Roche's men,' William replied, 'while I concentrated my efforts on the capture of Arthur of Brittany. We have him secure for the moment, but I seek your help in protecting him from the king's ire.'

'In what ways, and for what reason?' Hugh asked cautiously, in case this was a trap.

William lowered his voice. 'You have, I am told, been in John's immediate service for some time, and must therefore be no stranger to his wild rages. He is also merciless in victory, and has already sworn to have every noble prisoner dragged in chains across Normandy, barefoot, until their hapless families pay enough to recoup the cost incurred in needing to put down this pathetic rebellion. He has also made me responsible for Arthur's safety, since it was I who captured him, and I fear that at the slightest excuse he will have Arthur put to death, then cast the blame thereof on me.'

'And you wish for me to assist how?' Hugh asked.

'Merely by ensuring that Arthur is safely secured in a dungeon guarded by men loyal to both you and I. Two supplied by each of us, I suggest.'

Hugh thought briefly, then nodded. 'The security of such an important prisoner is clearly a grave matter, and I will be merely serving my master's best interests by assisting in it.'

'My thanks,' William replied, visibly relieved. 'I fear that young Arthur may prove to be the only one preserved from the wrath of the very Devil himself.'

There was little evidence of John's vengeful nature as he had himself admitted to Eleanor's chambers and knelt before her. 'I have delivered you from bondage like a true son,' he suggested smugly as he kissed her hand.

'Demonstrate also to the world that you are capable of mercy in victory. I am advised that there are many prisoners below whose only fault lay in following their own liege lords. While you may this day enjoy the fruits of victory, do all within your power to ensure that they do not become sour plums as the result of your thirst for revenge. Most particularly, do not harm a hair on the head of your nephew.'

'Will you not be here to ensure his safe keeping?' John asked.

Eleanor sighed. 'I am older than my years, John, and the events of recent days have only served to remind me that I am long overdue the veil. I shall take myself back to Fontevrault, there to realise my dream of taking holy orders. I shall pray for you, for your soul, and for the Aquitaine of my birth. Do nothing to require me also to pray for England. Now leave me, for I am weary of a life led surrounded by the blood of others.'

After only a brief delay, in order to allow his men to refresh themselves and enjoy the spoils of victory, John ordered a triumphant eastward march back into Normandy. Hugh was assigned the task of escorting Eleanor one final time to her chosen life in the cloisters of Fontevrault, after which he and his escort of fifty knights rode to join John inside the borders of Normandy at Falaise, where he learned that Angers was once again in English hands, following its capture by William des Roches, and that all the lands to the south-east of them now lay at peace for the first time since John's accession four years earlier.

Having reported to the Castellan of Falaise, Hubert de Burgh, and arranged for his immediate retinue to be lodged within the castle precincts, Hugh sought out William de Braose and enquired after the welfare of their high-born prisoner.

William smiled thinly, and replied, 'He is alive, and is at least being fed. Which is more than can be said for the poor souls we took prisoner at Mirebeau. They were all noble born, but have been herded like swine across the breadth of Anjou and Maine until we arrived here. Some have been shipped to English dungeons by way of Barfleur, and they may prove to be the lucky ones. John shows them no mercy, and several have died. Their families have petitioned Philip of France to sweep the English back across the Channel, and I fear that we may be invaded from the south ere long.'

'What says King John?' Hugh asked.

William gave an ironic laugh. 'Nothing — to those of us with his welfare as our greatest charge, anyway. Perhaps, were we lying on the pillow next to his head in the royal bedchamber instead of his ever-smiling wife, we might be heard when we attempt to counsel him to greater mercy. As it is, we do not see him before dinner, and are fortunate if he remains outside the bedchamber before the sun sets. Her Majesty must be gifted with many ways to engage the royal interest, since even simple lust expires once the deed is first done.'

Alarmed by what he was hearing, Hugh sought out Ranulf, who was perhaps the closest to John, and had been constantly by his side during the victorious attack on Mirebeau and its aftermath. The two men embraced, and Hugh looked searchingly into the eyes of his old friend as he asked, 'Is it true that John is showing no mercy to anyone?'

Ranulf nodded. 'Indeed he is not, and it is being muttered around the palace that some of those nobles who have only recently joined our side are contemplating desertion back to Philip. We shall be in a merry pickle if they do desert, leaving us with barely the men that we crossed over with a year since. It is also being rumoured that the fate of Brittany hangs on the same thread as the life of Prince Arthur.'

Hugh turned pale. 'What advice is John receiving in that regard?'

Ranulf shook his head as his lips formed a gesture of distaste. 'John hears what he wishes to hear. Following Arthur's refusal to bow down and accept the king as his overlord, insisting instead that *he* is the rightful King of England and Duke of Normandy, there are now some who whisper in John's ear that he should do away with Arthur, and by that means have the question resolved for all time.'

'Arthur was foolish enough to defy John, even while he is being held prisoner?'

Ranulf nodded. 'It's almost as if he wishes to die. Mind you, so might I, were I being held under such conditions.'

'But surely he remains a valuable bargaining piece with Philip of France?'

This time, Ranulf shook his head. 'Philip would seem to have abandoned him to his fate. All that keeps Arthur alive is the vigilance of those who can see that his death would be ruinous to John's cause. It is unfortunate that John does not see it that way.'

'He is thinking of having him put to death?'

'He would have done so already, had he been able to keep his hands clear of the stain of it. Arthur is being held prisoner by John, and all the rules of chivalry and honour require that he come to no harm while under his charge.'

'Then we need have no concerns for his welfare?' Hugh asked.

'Unless John can have someone else blamed for Arthur's death,' Ranulf pointed out.

The colour drained from Hugh's face. 'Two of my men are responsible for guarding his cell at all times, along with two supplied by William de Braose, who is the man appointed by John to ensure that Arthur does not escape. We would be the obvious ones to cast the blame upon, were ought to happen to Arthur whilst under our supervision.'

'That is why I am passing on the warning,' Ranulf replied. 'If those who urge John to do away with Arthur have their way, it will go badly for you. John would have your neck in order to prevent you denying any involvement.'

A very apprehensive Hugh spent the next three days passing backwards and forwards to the castle dungeons to reassure himself that Arthur was still alive, and threatening his men that if a violent hand was laid upon their prisoner they would pay for it with their lives. Then late on the afternoon of the fourth day he was visited by the Castellan of Falaise, Hubert de Burgh, with a blunt request that he remove his men from the dungeon corridor.

'I have been requested to have them there by William de Braose, who is the man charged by King John with the safety of Prince Arthur,' Hugh insisted.

De Burgh frowned with irritation. 'And *I* am charged with the security of the entire castle, Sir Hugh. It does not look good for the regard in which His Majesty holds me for such an important part of my castle to be guarded by others. I have raised the issue with King John himself, and it is his command that you remove your men. The same has been demanded of Sir William, who has taken it ill.'

'And you think that I will take it without demur?' Hugh replied testily.

'You might wish to enquire of the king himself, during those brief times when he is not ensconced with the queen.'

Opting to heed the unsubtle warning, Hugh made his way down several of the castle's dark, dank hallways until he reached the rooms allocated to William de Braose, only to be advised that he had ridden out late that afternoon, and had left word that he would not be returning. When he also learned that William des Roches had been granted leave to return to his estates in Anjou, but had instead ridden hard to the French Court and pledged his allegiance to King Philip, Hugh became very uneasy and demanded an audience with John. He was sitting in his chamber, thinking of Edwina and the children, late that same afternoon when the door flew open, and there stood John, minus any escort.

Hugh fell to his knees, only to be ordered back upright by a clearly bad-humoured John.

'I do not take kindly to being summoned to *your* presence, like some steward who has been caught pilfering the silver plate, but it so happens that I needed to speak with you anyway. De Burgh tells me that you took it ill when removed from guard duties over the prisoner Arthur of Brittany, despite it being on my orders.'

'Yes, sire, since I take my duties seriously, and did not wish ought to happen to the prisoner that might reflect badly on your good self. I responded the way I did because I undertake my duties as if guarding the lives of my own family.'

'That was *precisely* why you were replaced,' John said maliciously, adding, 'Do you have any drinkable wine in this pit of a chamber?'

Hugh poured two mugs of a passable *vin de Loire* with a trembling hand and awaited an explanation. John took a seat, and forced his face into what was intended as a reassuring smile, but still sent chills up and down Hugh's spine.

'It is to be rumoured abroad that Arthur has died,' John began. It was all Hugh could do to restrain himself from demanding to know what idiot had given that advice when John explained his reasoning further. 'We wish to test the reaction to those tidings, both in Brittany and in Paris. If they are not too adverse to our interests, we shall do nothing to dispel the rumour. But if the reactions are too clamorous, we shall produce the wretch for public view, very much alive. Then at least we shall know who our strongest enemies are.'

'But, sire, we are hardly well placed to resist any attack upon us from Paris,' Hugh argued. 'I am advised — or at least, it is rumoured — that des Roches has sided again with Philip, and I doubt that we can rely on the loyalties of de Braose any longer.

The remainder of our forces are paid by the day, and owe us no natural loyalty should the funds become depleted, and…'

He was silenced instantly by a raised hand from John, who glared and announced, 'I have ordered it, and it shall be done. You were replaced because your loyalty and known devotion to duty would have made rumours of Arthur's death less believable, and as for de Braose, he has been sent to parley with certain Welsh lords whose demands for freedom from taxation have become unacceptable.'

'If there is any unrest on the Welsh borders, I will need to defend my own estate, as will Ranulf of Chester,' Hugh pointed out.

John shook his head as he drained the rest of his wine, placed the mug on a nearby side table and walked to the door. 'I have spent long enough explaining how matters stand,' he said, 'although I still fail to see why I needed to explain myself to you. Rather the reverse. See to it that you and your men are ready to ride out two days hence, once the rumours circulate regarding Arthur's supposed death.'

'Might I enquire…?' Hugh began, to be silenced by another hand in the air.

'You might, and the answer is Rouen, there to be better positioned if Philip invades.'

# VII

The sudden transfer to Rouen proved to be a wise one, once the news got out that the young Duke of Brittany had been starved to death by William de Braose, who had since fled.

The whole of Brittany rose in rebellion, while nobles previously loyal to John publicly disavowed any ongoing loyalty to him. Philip of France hotly demanded that the Pope excommunicate John and place England under interdict, and Eleanor sent a blistering letter of condemnation of John's 'foul and blasphemous offence against both God and natural humanity'.

John hid himself away in the Palace of Rouen, drinking heavily from daybreak until late into the night, hurling foul invective against anyone who even attempted to raise items of State business with him, and calling down plagues on all those who appeared to have deserted his cause.

The only two members of the usual royal retinue who had been ordered to travel to Rouen were Hugh and Ranulf, and in the main it was their men who guarded the approaches to the castle from the River Seine, along which it was anticipated that any French forces might advance. They spent most of each day together, idly speculating on what John's next wild rage might produce in the way of an instruction, and wondering how their families might be faring without them, given the rumours of a threatened uprising by the Welsh.

Then one day Ranulf returned from his duties ashen-faced and barely speaking. Hugh leaped to his feet, pulled Ranulf into the chamber, closed the door, and led his old friend to the table, where he pressed a mug of wine into his trembling hand.

'What is it?' Hugh asked as his heart turned. 'Bad news from home?'

'No, thank God,' Ranulf finally managed to whisper hoarsely, 'but almost as bad.'

'What could possibly be as bad as that?'

'The murder of Arthur.'

'In what way?' Hugh reasoned. 'The world believes him to be dead anyway, so where is the added danger?'

Ranulf appeared to be struggling for the words, but eventually he murmured, 'It was John.'

'The king? How?'

'With his bare hands, or so my men advise me. They are pleading to be allowed home, before being taken up on some pretended charge and done away with in order to ensure their silence over what they witnessed.'

'When? How? Where?' was all that Hugh could manage.

'I was asked to supply the escort for a river trip along the Seine to the king's favoured manor house at Molineux. I queried why your men were not available for the task, and was advised that they were fully engaged on guard duties. I knew that not to be the case, but dared not argue, and in light of what happened I suspect that John was anxious regarding their honesty or something. Anyway, I sent Ralph and Gerald, and they tell me that no sooner had the boatman shipped the oars than a prisoner was led down to the water's edge and loaded into the boat. Ralph recognised him as Arthur, and assumed that they were transferring him to a safer place — I should perhaps confess that he was one of several men to whom I had told the truth regarding Arthur's continued life.'

'No mind to that, Ranulf,' Hugh insisted. 'For God's sake, tell me what happened!'

'According to Ralph — and Gerald supports his story — once the vessel was underway, John leaped upon Arthur, strangled him, then ran a dagger through his body several times and heaved his lifeless form over the side of the boat, weighed down with a large rock that had been in the scuppers of the boat all the while.'

'So John had planned his action — it was not just the result of another of his insane rages?'

'So it would seem. What in God's name are we to do?'

'You and I need do nothing,' Hugh counselled him, 'since we *know* nothing. It would be good were you to send your two men — Ralph and Gerald, you said their names were? — as far away from here as possible, for their own safety. Perhaps pretend that you have sent them to report on the state of our borders with the Welsh or something. But if they remain here, then without doubt their lives will be forfeit.'

'And you and I?'

'We remain at our posts, tight-lipped and outwardly unconcerned. We shall have enough to do, once Philip decides that the time is good to take back the Vexin and proceed up the Seine.'

They did not have long to wait long. As the winter of 1203 began in earnest, word was sent by way of an exhausted and terrified messenger that Philip of France was laying siege to the mighty fortress of Château Gaillard. Believing it to be impregnable, John ignored increasingly urgent advice from Hugh that even the most defendable of fortresses can be overrun when its occupants are starving. When Ranulf added that he was receiving reports from its castellan Roger de Lacy that the citizens of nearby Les Andelys were seeking shelter behind the walls of the château following depredations of their dwellings by French soldiers, John merely smiled and replied, 'This will make them more grateful that they are protected by John of England.'

Hugh tried to point out that the more people there were huddled behind the walls, the more quickly they'd use up whatever resources they had, and the greater the risk of an outbreak of disease.

John demanded, 'What know you of sieges, since you were never in the Holy Land?'

'I have seen as many sieges as Your Majesty has seen true friends, rather than sycophants who merely tell you what you want to hear!' Hugh retorted angrily.

'Leave my sight immediately, if you value your neck!' John bellowed as he hurled his wine mug at Hugh's head. It missed by a good few inches, bouncing off a statue of the late King Richard in what many took to be an ill omen.

Hugh pointed to the wine stain that was drizzling down the marble and yelled, 'At least *he* knew how to withstand a siege!' He then raced out before John could order that he be seized, and was found later by Ranulf, brooding darkly in a corner of his chamber.

'You are lucky not to be hanging from the walls,' Ranulf told him.

Hugh nodded. 'My advice was clearly not to his liking. Has he calmed down yet?'

'He's taken to his bedchamber again, so hopefully he will have forgotten by morning. But I suggest that you keep your head well below the parapet for the time being. *This* parapet, anyway — it may be needed inside Château Gaillard ere long.'

Philip of France was afforded the opportunity to demonstrate to the Christian world that he was more merciful than his rival when Roger de Lacy was left with no option but to evict over a thousand of the local citizens from the château as the winter wore on, and the supplies dwindled. They turned back in panic when they saw the besieging French forces advancing on them, only to find the château gates closed firmly behind them. Trapped between besieger and besieged, they could have died miserable deaths from either slaughter or starvation, but fortunately Philip himself arrived in time to order that they be fed, then allowed to return to what was left of their homes. Then, in a master stroke that owed much to his engineers, he succeeded in proving that Château Gaillard was not impregnable after all.

Like many a medieval castle, the château was served by a latrine chute down which human excrement and other unwanted waste could be launched. Demonstrating that what comes down can also go up, several nimble men at arms were sent to climb up the chute, and found themselves in the chapel. From there they slit a few unsuspecting throats and set fire to the heavy tapestries in order to create a diversion, during which they lowered the movable bridge over the moat and waved their comrades into the outer ward. After several retreats that left them cornered in the keep and almost bereft of further supplies, de Lacy gave the formal order to surrender, and Château Gaillard had now become an impregnable French base from which attacks could be launched down-river towards Rouen.

News of desertions now reached John's ears daily, although those who brought him news of yet more defections to Philip risked a blast of ill-tempered, and frequently drunken, rages, until only one man remained with the courage to attempt to drill the reality of his position into the king's seemingly impenetrable brain. That man was William Marshal, Earl of

Pembroke by dint of a crafty marriage, a knight-errant down to his heavily armoured sabatons.

He'd been a trusted military adviser since proving his worth alongside the former King Richard in the Crusade, and had led more than one successful raid into those provinces under the titular rule of John, whose barons had attempted rebellion, then learned the hard way that acquiescence was much easier. Once John came to appreciate that Hugh of Flint would only ever tell him things he didn't want to hear, he'd come to rely more and more on the dour wisdom of 'The Marshal', as everyone called him. William might be equally unwilling to tell John what he wanted to hear, but his growing reputation as a steely warrior who had never been known to retreat was a huge recommendation when it came to putting out fires of rebellion.

But this time even John had his doubts when Marshal urged him to withdraw back across the Channel and leave him to travel to Paris and secure some sort of treaty with Philip.

'Why should I do that, thereby falsely signalling weakness?' John demanded.

Marshall shook his head as if correcting a squire on the stance to adopt when facing an opponent. 'You would be underlining your strength, sire,' he assured him. 'With the Channel between you and Philip, you can rebuild your army with a view to returning in full battle order. At present, given recent defections, we have lost Saumur, Coutances, Falaise, Bayeux, Caen…'

'Yes, yes!' John cut him off with an impatient wave. 'I need no reminder of those yellow-faced chicken livers who have let the French bastard walk all over them. Should you not be hacking them down in my name?'

'Better to attack the head than the limbs, sire,' Marshal replied gravely. 'If I can persuade Philip that he has neither the resources, nor the time, to hold down so many hostile territories, then we shall win ourselves the time to regroup. We may then return to Normandy in triumph, with you at our head, and sweep all resistance aside.'

John still looked doubtful. 'And I must retreat to England, say you?'

'Not "retreat", sire — merely withdraw as a matter of strategy, while I remain and conduct the diplomacy.'

'And what of Ranulf of Chester — does he not occupy the role of ambassador to the French?'

'And has he succeeded thus far?' Marshal challenged him. When John shook his head, Marshal reinforced his argument with diplomacy. 'He was a wise choice before weapons were drawn, but now it requires a man of military experience and determination.'

John sighed. 'It shall be as you wish. But who will escort me back, while you journey south?'

Marshal gritted his teeth. 'Although Earl Hugh of Flint has recently been guilty of grave errors of the mouth, have you ever known him fail you with his sword arm?'

John's eyes flashed angrily, but then he appreciated the wisdom of what was being suggested. 'Indeed not. So you suggest that he be the one to escort me back to England?'

'I can think of none better, sire. And you might opt to travel back with the Earl of Chester, who may do what he does best in persuading your Council and your subjects to raise the finance for your triumphant return here.'

An hour later Marshal found Hugh and Ranulf at supper, and lost no time in advising them of his success. 'I have finally persuaded the arrant fool to return to England before the damage grows any greater. If the reports that have begun to reach me of how matters stand over there are accurate, you will both find your differing talents stretched to the utmost.'

It was hardly a triumphal homecoming. Given the uprising in Brittany, John and his reduced retinue had deemed it safer to escape by way of Le Havre, and from there follow the predominant westerly wind to Dover. There was a hurried debate regarding whether or not to strike north immediately for London. However, the sullen faces of those who watched the royal vessels being unloaded persuaded those in John's immediate company that it would not be good for his current state of depression, interspersed with outbreaks of violent anger, to be reminded of the disgrace that many believed he had brought to the image of England as a warring nation.

They therefore headed to Canterbury, where they would at least be assured of a friendly welcome by its archbishop, Hubert Walter, who was also still Justiciar of England. It was a miserable Christmas, during which John caused considerable embarrassment to Walter by railing loudly against God, casting doubts on the Resurrection, and claiming that his authority as king could not be challenged by any earthly power, nor put on a lower pedestal of reverence than any so-called biblical prophet or alleged representative of God.

This scandalised the monks of Canterbury, who regarded John's outbursts as sacrilegious and blasphemous at best, and John himself as some sort of anti-Christ. This was to have long-term consequences when Archbishop Walter died the following year, and a schism developed regarding his successor.

John was equally scathing and critical of anyone who failed to do his bidding, for whatever reason, and two manifestations of this related to the recent loss of most of John's possessions across the Channel. First was the apparent defection of

William Marshal to the French camp, and the second was the loss of the castle of Le Vaudreuil in Normandy.

Marshal had been left in Normandy as the final line of communication with the advancing French army. He was well respected by his enemies as both a vigorous warrior and a man of chivalric honour, and John hoped to stem the flood of the French tide across his former territories by means of a peace treaty. William retained a Norman estate in Tancarville, a few miles east of Le Havre. When he was commissioned by John to approach Philip of France, William was given permission to swear allegiance to Philip for his Norman estate in tandem with his corresponding allegiance to John.

When news reached Canterbury that William had been obliged to pay exclusive homage to Philip in order to retain his Norman possessions, John was incandescent with rage, loudly accusing Marshal of treachery, treason and dishonour. It was hardly surprising that Marshal opted to remain in Normandy until the fire of John's wrath had been allowed to fizzle out, and when the crushing news was brought to John in April of 1204 that his mother Eleanor had died, seemingly bereft of her reason, in her self-imposed cell in Fontevrault, he felt unable to instruct Marshal to attend her funeral as the sole representative of the last of her sons.

In the midst of all this misery, John was hardly likely to be well disposed towards the two men he had left as Joint Governors of Vaudreuil Castle, south of Rouen, when they surrendered it to Philip's massive siege force on the first summons to do so. Rouen had still been in English hands when John and the royal party had abandoned it, with strict orders to those left to guard the last vestiges of English occupation of the Duchy that they should fight to the last man. The two men who relinquished Vaudreuil without a blow being struck were Robert FitzWalter and Saer de Quincy, and they were held as prisoners by a gleeful Philip of France until their families could ransom them. Far from giving financial assistance for the release of those he had left behind to feel the full might of the French enemy, John accused the two men of cowardice, and the drastic financial burden placed upon their respective families was to rankle with FitzWalter for many years.

Hugh was closely confined to Canterbury, resentful of not being able to return, even briefly, to his family in order to reassure them that he was still alive. He was also feeling the absence of his friend and confidant Ranulf of Chester, who had been sent on an exploratory mission around the nation in order to assess its mood. Hugh therefore leaped at the chance when instructed by John to venture north, via Rochester, into London. He was to assess the prospect of raising finance by way of taxation of its merchants; the money would then be used to employ mercenaries to re-take Normandy.

On first arriving in London he attempted to contact those of the Council who might be able to assist him, but was alarmed to learn that it had not met for months, and that most of its leading members had returned to their country estates. When he made enquiry of such senior clerks as he could find still working in half-empty State offices, such as those of the Treasury and Chancery, he was advised that the barons who had originally been honoured with a seat on John's Council had either travelled with him, as in the case of William Marshal, or had established themselves outside London, as had Hubert Walter in his other capacity as Archbishop of Canterbury.

But, more ominously, several leading deserters from Council had let it be known that they felt irrelevant, powerless and forgotten during John's lengthy and largely disastrous overseas expedition. They were also tired of his acquisition of sycophantic 'familiares', who reassured him that he was a warrior king hewn from the same rich ore as his father and older brother. In the main these hangers-on were minor nobles from Poitou who had purported to be mercenaries bringing bodies of fighting men into his retinue, whereas the sad reality was that they were effete nonentities basking in the reflected glow of royalty. More than one of those talented public servants on whom John should have been able to rely had deserted their posts in disgust.

Hugh's first, and only, meeting with the Mayor of London Henry FitzAilwin was both brief and depressing. He assured Hugh that the king's inability to ensure safe passage for English cloth across Flanders into the Low Countries threatened to bankrupt most of those in the city who relied in some way or other on the garment trade. Therefore, any attempt to raise money by an additional port tax, cloth levy or warehouse tithe would be likely to lead to an armed uprising. Thoroughly disheartened, Hugh persuaded himself that he had earned a few weeks of relaxation among family and friends.

His first visit was on his way north, to the estate at Repton that his much younger brother Robert had inherited from their father after Hugh had been awarded the Earldom of Flint by the late King Richard. As Hugh had anticipated, Robert and his wife Beth now had three children, ranging in age from twelve downwards, so the estate was well provided with managers for the foreseeable future. Robert gave a cheer as he saw Hugh dismounting and walked over to embrace him after calling for ale and bread to be brought outside. Then he invited Hugh to take a seat under the portico and enquired how long he would be staying.

'One night only, I'm afraid, since I'm anxious to get back to my own family,' Hugh replied. 'How goes the estate?'

'Middling well,' Robert said, 'but no thanks to the weather and the prices. The harvests have never improved since the days of the last king, and the incessant demands from the current one for scutage to pay for his wars in foreign parts have left most of us tight for seed and other necessities. I take it that you are still in the royal service?'

'I am,' Hugh confirmed, 'but I wish I were not. King John will not listen to those of us who know what warfare is about, and as a result England has lost most of its foreign possessions while John remains surrounded by fools who tell him only what he wants to hear. How fare your friends in the Shire Wood?'

'Most of them have returned to the lands they once farmed before John threw them off after the really bad famine of those former years. At least we now have a half decent sheriff — ah, here comes our dinner.'

Beth came out with a broad smile as she laid the board between their feet. 'How are Edwina and the children?' she asked.

Hugh spread his arms. 'I have not seen them these past two years or so, such has been the extent of my service alongside the king, but I am on my way home now, which is why I shall abide here for only one night.'

'You're welcome to stay for as long as you wish,' Beth replied, 'but tell that king of yours to stop levying taxes on poor folk such as us.'

Hugh smiled. 'You are at least rich in happiness, which is a commodity that many would give all they have in order to possess. But is that a sentiment that is broadly held in these parts?' he asked as he turned back to Robert. 'That you are over-taxed?'

'In *all* parts, I would imagine,' Robert replied. 'It would not be so bad if we believed that the money was being well spent. Are the rumours true, that King John lost all his lands across the Channel because he spent too long in bed?'

Hugh laughed lightly, hoping to take the sting out of the accusation. 'There were many factors at play, but it is true that he and the new queen are well suited in the bedchamber.'

'But there are, as yet, no heirs?' Robert asked.

Hugh shook his head. 'Not when I left the Court, anyway.'

'That's perhaps as well,' Robert observed. 'When we are rid of this cursed family from abroad, and have a king with the true interests of England at heart, matters might improve on estates such as this.'

As Hugh lay down to sleep that night, the pleasant thought that he was only three days at most from home and family was marred somewhat by what Robert had said about the Angevin dynasty that had ruled England for so many years. He had a lurking feeling that he was probably correct.

# VIII

Hugh dismounted a hundred yards back from the manor house door. He then walked his horse as silently as possible towards the young boy who had his back to him as he slashed at a stuffed sack hanging from a tree branch on the grass strip in front of the house. He was armed with a stout stick, and the sack was much the worse for wear as the result of his dedicated punishment of it.

Hugh grinned as he recalled his own early youth, when he would engage in precisely the same activity, but without anyone to guide him since he grew up with a lawyer for a father. That father had gone on to achieve great things during the reign of the former King Richard, and Hugh hoped that he had done him proud. As for this nine-year-old stripling, there was much that *his* father could teach him.

The lad took a break from hacking at his opponent while he regained his breath, and Hugh took the opportunity to shout advice.

'Remember always to thrust *forward* into your opponent,' he yelled. 'If you slash like a man bailing hay, you are obliged to raise your sword arm, and a skilful adversary can come under your armpit, where there is no armour to protect you.'

The lad turned, and a broad smile spread across his face as he threw down his weapon and ran towards Hugh's open arms.

'Father!' he yelled. 'You are returned unharmed! We heard that many had been lost fighting in Normandy, and we were fearful until Uncle Ranulf called in to reassure us that you were safe. Welcome home!'

Hugh gripped his son in a bear hug and fought back the tears. Then he stepped back and took a long look at the boy who would one day become the Second Earl of Flint.

'You have grown apace. Mother must be feeding you well.'

'Not Mother — Nan. She feeds and looks after us all, despite her years.'

'She doesn't stop you from attacking bags filled with soil, though,' Hugh said. 'For all her attention, it might have fallen on your head, had you succeeded in dislodging it.'

'She watches from the house,' Geoffrey assured him, 'although she tries not to let me see her.'

As if to prove his point, Nan came through the front door carrying little Edith in her arms. She saw Hugh, called back inside the manor house, then put the two-year-old down on her feet and told her, 'Here's Dada!'

Hugh felt the lump rising in his throat as he gazed lovingly at the little girl on wobbly legs who stood looking at him with big, dark eyes that widened in fear as he walked towards her with open arms. When he was only a few feet away, she gave a startled squawk and turned back towards Nan, leaping into her arms as the old lady leaned down to collect her. Once installed in the safest place she knew, Edith began sucking her thumb and glaring at Hugh as if to defy him to come any closer.

'At least *I'm* glad to see you home safe!' Edwina called as she rushed from the door into Hugh's arms, adding, 'Even if you *do* need to wash. As for poor little Edith, she's no idea who you are, and you can hardly blame her for that. How long has it been this time?'

'Almost two years,' he admitted, 'but there was much to occupy us in Normandy.'

'There isn't now, if the rumours be true,' Edwina replied. 'Now, come inside and have something to eat. *After* you've washed, that is.'

'So what rumours have you heard?' Hugh asked after complimenting Nan on her venison pasties and reminding himself that elderflower wine made from the flowers in his own hedgerows was just as good as any French beverage.

Edwina frowned. 'They may not be mere rumours, since they came from a reliable source — someone who should know. He wants to meet with you, by the way.'

'Who is he? Why does he wish to meet with me? And what has he been saying?'

'First part first,' she insisted. 'Is it true that all the English lands across the Channel have been lost because the king wouldn't leave his bed, except for long enough to murder his own nephew with both hands? And that he is now planning to tax the people in order to hire soldiers to win back the lands that he lost through laziness? If so, you must be in deep disgrace as a knight in his service. Is that why you are returned home? Have you been exiled from Court?'

Hugh sighed. 'It's true that we have lost most of our lands overseas, although when I left we still had a foothold in Normandy, and William Marshal was sent to parley truce terms with Philip of France. But it is true that we lost Anjou, Maine, Aquitaine and Brittany, leaving only Poitiers. You should also know that Queen Dowager Eleanor has died.'

'Of embarrassment, presumably,' Edwina commented sourly. 'You mentioned Brittany — what do you know of the fate of Prince Arthur?'

Hugh looked carefully around before lowering his voice and replying, 'Only what Ranulf tells me, and even *that* is what he heard from two of his men. It seems that John did away with the boy with his bare hands, then threw him into the Seine, weighed down with a rock. But *please* do not spread that information around, else it will go ill for Ranulf.'

'He was here briefly, some weeks ago now,' Edwina recalled. 'He was much taken with Geoffrey, since he has no children of his own, and I believe that he wishes to approach you with a view to taking our son into his household, to be tutored in courtly manners.'

'That might be a wise move, once I have taught him how to fight,' Hugh nodded.

Edwina grabbed him by the wrist in protest. 'You will do no such thing! Bad enough that I have to worry about a husband who risks his life in the service of a fool, without the heartache of an only son engaged in the same madness!'

'He may not prove to be our *only* son,' Hugh leered meaningfully, to a responding snort from Edwina.

'He will be if you do not mend your ways. I have grown quite accustomed to sleeping alone, so be warned.'

Nan gave a diplomatic cough as she entered the hall with a fruit platter, and Edwina's face reddened with embarrassment. Hugh took the opportunity to ask, 'So who has been seeking me, other than Ranulf, that is?'

'Ranulf has journeyed north,' she told him, 'but the man who wishes to meet with you is equally responsible for the safety of this portion of the nation. He is the Constable of Chester, although quite where he obtains his authority from is a mystery to me. Isn't Ranulf the Earl of Chester?'

'He is, but the duty of guarding strategic castles is one imposed on men who have proved themselves in battle, whereas earls such as Ranulf are elevated because of their favouritism with the king. In Ranulf's case, he inherited a title that goes all the way back to the conquest of England by

William of Normandy, but even his best friend would hesitate to call him a warrior. Hence the need to have a strategic fortress such as Chester commanded by a man of warfare. So who *is* the man I must journey to meet?'

'He gave the name "Roger de Lacy", as I recall,' Edwina replied, 'and he said that you and he fought with King Richard in Outremer. I must own that I do not recall him from those days.'

'I most certainly do, although I never got beyond Cyprus, as you may remember,' Hugh said. 'But more recently he withstood the siege of Château Gaillard, in Normandy, for almost eight months. Philip of France finally overran it using trickery rather than by military might, but I'm surprised that de Lacy wasn't deprived of all his titles, since his defeat was the end of our ambitions in Normandy, and John would have been looking for someone to blame.'

'Well, he was here barely two weeks ago,' Edwina assured him, 'although he would not say why. When I advised him that you were with King John in Normandy, he seemed to think that you would not be long in returning, and asked that you call and see him at your convenience.'

'So I will, once I have rested. For the time being, tell me how our daughter fares. She clearly took me for a robber or something, and I must take steps to reassure her that I mean her only love. She has your beautiful black hair, and your deep brown eyes; she will have a line of suitors when she reaches womanhood.'

'And you will no doubt sell her off to the highest bidder, or some fat old noble with large estates,' Edwina replied with distaste. 'I was lucky to be able to choose who I wedded, although there have been times recently when I wondered if I had chosen wisely. An absent husband is worse than no husband at all.'

'This time I hope to be home for some weeks,' he reassured her. 'The king has bid me journey the length and breadth of the realm to sound out prospects for further taxes with which to pay for mercenary soldiers in order to reclaim his overseas estates.'

'Then he will not require *your* services, will he?' Edwina asked hopefully.

Hugh smiled. 'You clearly know nothing of warfare. Mercenary soldiers require strong commanders to keep them in order.'

'And wives require constant husbands to protect and nurture them,' Edwina replied shortly. 'Have you eaten enough? If so, perhaps you might wish to remind me of those things I was deprived of for two years that felt more like ten.'

Two weeks later Hugh reminded himself that the mighty Chester Castle had been built for defence rather than comfort as he urged his tired mount up the steep grassy slope towards its wooden palisade and intimidating double gates. Beyond the palisade was a single tower, square in design and built from stone, that promised little in the way of spacious interior chambers or welcoming banquet halls.

The gate guard had him conveyed by a bulky man at arms to the main door of the tower keep, where he repeated his identity and the general nature of his business. He was told to go back outside and await further instruction, and after an hour he was beginning to tire of the view of the bustling town below and the River Dee that, half a day's ride west, formed the northern boundary of his own estate. Then a head appeared through the keep door and ordered him gruffly inside, where he was escorted, in the manner of a high-born prisoner, down a corridor to the door of an inner chamber. A command to enter followed the heavy knock on the sturdy wooden door, and Hugh was ushered into a small and gloomy room whose only furnishings consisted of a heavy oak table and several chairs on either side of it. There was a fire burning fitfully in a grate in the corner, and the desk was strewn with scrolls. The man behind the table rose and nodded Hugh into a chair without offering to shake his hand.

'I recall your face from those gathered in the company of our king in Rouen, before I was despatched to command Gaillard,' the man announced by way of welcome, 'and like myself, you seem to have survived being in the royal service.'

'I was in Rouen when the château fell,' Hugh replied cautiously. 'You are lucky to have survived the king's wrath.'

De Lacy smiled. 'He relies on me to keep out the Welsh, and the château would still be ours if John had sent an army to raise the siege. An army that might well have been led by you, I assume.'

'There *was* no army,' Hugh replied, as much in his own defence as John's. 'The funds had run out, and his largely mercenary force had deserted. I was there merely to guard his person, and we made a run for Le Havre shortly thereafter.'

'Were you there when Arthur was murdered?' de Lacy asked.

Hugh thought quickly before replying, 'He died naturally, in Falaise, while being held prisoner.'

'Do not think to pass off that nonsense on me,' de Lacy replied testily. 'Would it assist your memory if I told you that I recently received a visit from your good friend and neighbour Ranulf of Chester?'

'I know not what Ranulf told you, but we were advised that Arthur died in Falaise,' Hugh insisted. 'Whatever the manner of his death, it is a fact that he is dead, so why should we concern ourselves how that came about?'

'Because,' de Lacy replied coldly, 'the blame is being laid at the feet of William de Braose, who was responsible for Arthur's safekeeping.'

'And I can confirm that de Braose was sent from the Court at Rouen in order to assess the state of the Welsh Marches. He was gone at least a week before Arthur died.'

He regretted his incautious words the minute they left his mouth, and de Lacy gave a grin of triumph.

'At least you no longer maintain the lie that Arthur died in Falaise. This attests to your honesty, not to mention your loyalty to the Earl of Chester. I hope that I can trust you with further intelligence.'

'That will rather depend upon what it is,' Hugh replied guardedly, 'bearing in mind that I am a loyal servant of King John.'

'Are you not perhaps a more loyal servant of England?' de Lacy asked.

'That is the same thing,' Hugh said.

'But *is* it?' de Lacy challenged him. 'If your true loyalty lies with England, how can you sit by while John brings the nation into such disrepute, while bankrupting it in order to fight an opponent who is much cleverer than him? Is it not time for those who truly strive for England's good fortune to insist on being better consulted, and less heavily taxed, while those fools who surround the throne line up at the royal trough like the greedy swine that they are?'

Hugh was taken aback by such mutinous talk, and it showed in his face. De Lacy caught the look and challenged him further.

'You think perhaps that I speak treason? Sedition? Disloyalty to the throne? I speak for the future of England, Hugh, and it will *have* no future unless John listens to those with wise counsel. Those flopgiblets from Poitou with whom he surrounds himself will simply guess what so-called "advice" will earn them the greatest reward, keep them closer to the seat of power, and assure them of a soft lifestyle at Court. Those who seek to keep John's nose to the grindstone of reality, and would fight alongside him for the future of England, are cast out into the wilderness with wicked lies. These are the very men who defend our wives and families from not only the French, but the Welsh and Scots, who would invade without hesitation if they knew of the parlous state that England is really in, thanks to John.'

He finally fell silent, while Hugh tried to take it all in. He was being asked to add his name to a rebellion of some sort, that was clear, but before rejecting it out of hand he would need to consider its merits. It was true that John rejected counsel that he found unpalatable, as Hugh had learned to his cost more than once. It was equally true that England had been driven out of its foreign estates by a French king who knew precisely how to play the arrogant, self-justifying and vain youngest son of his old enemy. But something de Lacy had said had alarmed him.

'What of the Welsh, say you?' he asked. 'Are they set to invade?'

'Not yet,' de Lacy reassured him, 'but that is only due to the ongoing strength and loyalty of men whom John does not deserve to have on his side. I already mentioned that William de Braose is being spoken of abroad — in rumours that originate from John — as the one who brought about the death of Prince Arthur, and by this means brought the French down on our heads. William is one of our most important bulwarks against the Welsh princes, given his estates in Powys and Gower. Likewise, of course, your estate in Flint and those of Ranulf here in Chester. Fortresses such as the one in which we are seated today are intended to serve as bases from which to suppress any Welsh uprising, and yet John risks our loyalty by accusing us of acts of incompetence or disloyalty so that we may take the blame for his misdeeds. It cannot continue in this manner, if England is to remain defended by men loyal to its cause.'

'And this was why you summoned me here?' Hugh asked. 'To test my loyalty to John?'

'No, your loyalty to England. Ranulf has judged you aright.'

'And what did he say of me, precisely?' Hugh demanded.

'That you were steadfast in your loyalties, devoted to your family and your estate, but stubborn to the point of rebellion for what you believe to be right. I am also advised that your father displayed similar traits that ultimately cost him his life. Like you, it seems that he thought more of England than he did of currying favour with John.'

'So what do you require of me?' Hugh asked, not sure if he was prepared for any answer he might receive.

'Nothing — as yet — except to continue in your loyalty to Chester, and remain ready to strike a blow for England.'

'Against whom?'

'Anyone who threatens it, either by armed aggression or vainglorious stupidity. They are equally dangerous for the nation. And so I bid you a very good day.'

It was not until Hugh was riding home that the full import of the conversation struck him. The man had clearly trusted him to the extent of admitting that he was preparing a rebellion against the king if he felt that he needed to do so for the sake of the nation. The more he thought about it, the more Hugh was reluctantly obliged to concede that what de Lacy had said not only made perfect sense, but accorded very closely with what he himself believed deep down. He might well have to place personal safety to one side if John continued to blunder from one disastrous decision to another.

As he rode down the track towards Flint Manor House, he waved at the small group sitting under the portico enjoying wine and wafers. Alongside Edwina was the familiar, and welcome, figure of Ranulf, and proudly displaying his skill with a cup and ball was Geoffrey, prancing around the grass strip. Little Edith looked up from Edwina's lap as she heard the horse approaching and called out 'Dada', as she had finally learned to do in the brief time he'd been home. She still didn't know what the word meant, but she knew that the person to whom it belonged was a nice man who gave her lots of cuddles.

'Are you here to steal my family from me?' Hugh asked jokingly as he dismounted and handed the reins to the groom.

Ranulf smiled back. 'Rather I am here to steal you from your family. I think I've convinced Edwina that it's not your fault this time.'

'That doesn't make it any more acceptable,' Edwina frowned, 'but at least I know that you'll be in good company.'

'Until we reach London, anyway,' Hugh replied, then turned to Ranulf. 'I take it that's where we are bound?'

'John has not commanded it, but it's time that we showed our faces back down there.'

'Do you think that John even noticed our absence?' Hugh asked the following morning as they trotted down the long track that led towards Lichfield and beyond.

Ranulf chuckled. 'Probably not, although he may just recall that he sent you to enquire regarding the prospect for more taxation, so that we may strike back at Philip across the Channel.'

'Asking the barons if they are prepared to consent to more taxes is surely like requiring hens to invite a fox to supper in the henhouse?' Hugh jested, and turned when he heard no responding chuckle from his companion.

Ranulf's face was unreadable as he asked, 'Did you speak with de Lacy?'

'I did,' Hugh confirmed, 'and in many ways I wish I hadn't.'

'But did you agree with him?'

'Regarding *what*, precisely?' Hugh hedged. 'How can you know what we talked about?'

'Because he and I had a similar conversation on my return from the North, where I went to enquire regarding the state of our borders with the Scots. I will be obliged to advise the king that his leading nobles up there will not contribute another brass penny towards his madness across the Channel.'

'John will not be pleased with your tidings, assuming that you report back accurately.'

'I shall tell him, out of loyalty and a sense of duty, what he needs to hear, even if it means I lose my head.'

'He will not find anyone prepared to lay hands on you, Ranulf — least of all me.'

'That is what I was hoping to hear,' Ranulf replied, across the heads of the two horses as their brasses jangled in unison. 'I believe that we are both set on a course that can only be best for England, even if it makes widows of our wives.'

# IX

As Hugh and Ranulf entered the Audience Chamber inside Westminster Palace, they were almost bowled over by the hasty exit of a very red-faced cleric whose wattled cheeks flapped with indignation like the wings of a goose about to take flight. John was still chuckling at his own wit as he beckoned the two newcomers to his raised throne dais.

'You just missed the emissary from the Prior of Canterbury Cathedral, who wishes me to support the cause of its sub-prior to be elected as their new archbishop,' he told them. 'I sent him back with a message inviting his prior to shove one of his altar candles up his holy arse. You have presumably learned of the death of Hubert Walter?'

'Indeed, sire,' Hugh replied cheekily. 'It's the talk of the kitchens.'

Ranulf kicked Hugh's ankle in warning, and John glared at the impudence, but fortunately was more concerned regarding what they had to report.

'More of that in due course, since I maintain the sole right to appoint the next archbishop. Now, what have you to report regarding the state of the Welsh Marches?'

'They remain secure, sire,' Ranulf replied. 'It would seem that Llywelyn of Gwynedd is content within his boundaries, and is honoured to have been offered your daughter Joan as a wife.'

Both men held their breath in case John took offence at this reference to an illegitimate daughter allegedly sired by him during his time in Normandy, but his mind was clearly on other matters.

'What of de Braose? Has he secured his boundaries sufficiently, think you?'

'I am no military man, sire, as you are aware,' Ranulf replied deferentially, 'but all seemed to be as it should be.'

'I want him carefully watched,' John growled, 'since it was thanks to his laxity in guarding and seeing to the welfare of my dear nephew Arthur that I lost a close family member.'

Ranulf gave an involuntary gasp at the sheer effrontery of this claim, then attempted to convert it into a cough as John glared at him.

'Do you claim to know otherwise?' he demanded, and when Ranulf shook his head silently, John continued in a low, warning voice. 'I had occasion to have two of your men consigned to the Tower after their desertion of their posts at Rouen. It seems that before they fled, they reported having seen Prince Arthur on a boat on the Seine. That cannot be, can it?'

'Indeed not, sire,' Ranulf replied meekly, 'unless they saw his ghost. It is well established that Prince Arthur died at Falaise, hence your discontent with de Braose.'

'Indeed,' John said sadistically, 'but you must take steps to ensure that no more idle rumours circulate of Arthur being seen in Rouen. We understand each other, I hope?'

'Indeed we do, sire,' Ranulf replied as he let out a sigh of relief. 'But returning to the state of the Welsh Marches, I repeat that happily they remain secure. I also took the opportunity to visit the Constable at Chester Castle, and he reports that they are at full strength, and well prepared to meet any planned incursion from Wales.'

'This is good,' John replied, 'since we must look to our southern boundaries, and in particular focus our attention on defending the Channel against invasion. I have given orders that the sea defences of the Cinque Ports be doubled, and that we increase the number of vessels available for an invasion of our own to reclaim the lands seized by Philip, beginning with Poitou. This will of course require money, and I have ordered the Chancery to impose another scutage tax. We currently have no Chancellor following Walter's death, but that is all to the good, since I can manage the financial affairs of the nation in person, without dithering officials attempting to advise me against those things I must do in the interests of the nation. Hugh, what did you learn of the current mood among the barons regarding the state of the realm?'

Hugh coughed politely and hoped that the words he had been rehearsing for days would sound suitably convincing. 'In the main, and to report truthfully, sire, they are concerned at the loss of our possessions abroad, since many of them, as you will be aware, own estates themselves in our former duchies such as Normandy, Maine, Anjou and Aquitaine. As for Poitou, as you yourself will be aware, given the presence at your Court of Poitevin nobles such as Gerard d'Athies, Engelard de Cigogné, and…'

'Stop drivelling, man!' John yelled. 'What will be the likely response of the lazy scum who sat back while I defended their estates abroad? Speak plainly!'

Since the plain truth was probably the last thing John really wished to hear, Hugh drew a deep breath, said a silent prayer and replied, 'They do not wish to be taxed further, sire.'

'Ungrateful bastards!' John yelled. 'Idle cowards! Yellow-livered milksops! They expect me to fight their battles for them, but withhold the funds with which to do it? Do they fondly imagine that the useless God to whom they throw money for prayers for their souls will somehow descend and smite their enemies? It is *I* upon whom they depend, *I* who will preserve their lands, and *I* who require the means to do so! Perhaps I should begin distraining on their lands, or holding their wives and children hostage, until they get the message! Go back and tell them that either they pay, or they will be thrown off their lands to earn an honest living as millers or blacksmiths.'

'Yes, sire,' Hugh muttered, 'but they will take it ill.'

'And I will take it ill if they do not pay!' John thundered. 'Now, the matter of William Marshal.'

'What of him, sire?' Ranulf asked.

John's face set in an expression of distaste. 'I fear he may have deserted to the side of Philip of France. He was last heard of in Évreux, where I believe you have family connections, Ranulf.'

'Indeed, sire, since my mother is of the House of de Montfort. Her name is Bertrade, and I believe that you and she are distant cousins.'

'Very distant,' John replied with a frown, 'which is why I wish you to renew some family acquaintances.'

'Sire?'

'I wish you to journey to Évreux in search of William Marshal and sound out his loyalties. If he has gone over to France, then make your excuses and leave; if not, advise him that he is required back at my Court, on pain of losing his estates of Pembroke and Leinster. His wife remains in Ireland, but she is a de Clare. Her nephew Richard has lesser estates in Tonbridge, and would dearly love to get his hands on her vast estates should I have her thrown off them due to Marshal's defection. You might advise him of that when and if you meet with him.'

Ranulf looked aghast. 'It is your wish that I travel alone through lands that now belong to England's enemies, in an attempt to persuade one of Philip's allies, and a mighty warrior in his own right, to defect from Philip's service and return to England?'

'You fear for your own safety?'

'Would *you* not?' Ranulf asked, then reddened when he realised what he had just said. 'What I mean is, sire, that a lesser man such as myself, with no military training or skill…'

'Yes, yes, spare me the coward's excuse,' John replied curtly. 'If you are so concerned for your head, take the Earl of Flint with you. He's been known to cut off a few in his time.'

'Sire,' Hugh objected when he contemplated the prospect of another lengthy sojourn away from home, 'you have already commissioned me to travel the nation in order to persuade the barons of the importance of paying taxes. I have not yet completed that mission.'

'That can wait,' John replied. 'The barons should not need any reminder of their feudal obligations to their king. If they do, then it will take the form of forfeiture of their estates to others more prepared to acknowledge their value. You will ride to Évreux with the Earl of Chester.'

They travelled as unobtrusively as they could as they headed steadily south through Normandy. They were armed, but dressed as travellers in plain garments, as they passed themselves off as mercenaries on their way to offer their services to the King of France. They avoided the larger population centres and stayed at country inns, eating and drinking sparingly and retiring early to their shared chamber every night.

As they slowly made their way south towards the Vexin, they took the opportunity to exchange opinions, hopes, aspirations and fears, not the least of which concerned the state into which England was rapidly descending.

'Even if we do succeed in meeting up with William Marshal,' Hugh observed gloomily, 'I cannot anticipate that he'll be persuaded to return to England, given the mentality of its current ruler.'

Ranulf grunted in agreement before adding, 'Perhaps the threat of the loss of his estates will prove to be the inducement that John intended.'

'And perhaps not,' Hugh countered. 'He was a mere knight — albeit one of the best — before Richard consented to his marriage to Isabel de Clare. She was but a girl, while he was approaching fifty years of age, and legend has it that he was more interested in her body than her lands. Certainly she seems to have borne a child for almost every year of their marriage, then for some reason he all but abandoned her in Ireland. My point is that William Marshal is a man whose actions and motives cannot be easily predicted. He may well have reasons of his own for wishing to remain in France, and will not be easily brought to heel by threats from John. But he may well have moved on from Évreux.'

'It is to be hoped not,' Ranulf replied, 'since I look forward to meeting my mother's family and learning more about my ancestry. This said, ours is not the only house to be linked by marriage to the de Montforts. The current Earl of Leicester, Robert de Beaumont, has a sister called Amicia, who is married to the current Lord of Montfort-l'Amaury, which is the other main Montfort estate, barely a day's ride from Paris itself.'

Hugh chuckled. 'It is obviously of great advantage to have a foot in both camps. As I seem to recall from what my father told me of his time with King Henry, the de Montforts were able to ride both horses, in a manner of speaking, by paying homage to the French King for Montfort-l'Amaury, while entertaining English kings at Évreux. If it comes to that, I was told that my parents were married at Évreux — it seems to be well suited to the joining of houses.'

'On the subject of families,' Ranulf replied tentatively, 'did Edwina mention my offer to take Geoffrey into my household? As you know, Clemence and I have no children of our own, and it would please me greatly to have a young man at my side to raise in the Courtly ways. With you passing on to him your martial skills, he will be well prepared to take his place among the finest at the English Court.'

'If it remains English,' Hugh muttered darkly. 'The way matters are heading, it may degenerate into merely a branch of the Court of Poitiers, or — God forbid — it may become a mere arm of the French crown. As to your offer, I shall of course discuss it with Geoffrey — and Edwina.'

'I think that Edwina's will prove to be the deciding voice,' Ranulf chuckled, 'and I have already persuaded her, unless I miss my mark in the matter.'

Hugh thought long and hard. He'd been on the point of raising the issue more than once while in Ranulf's company, but had always shrunk from doing so. Now it somehow seemed appropriate. He cleared his throat nervously. 'In point of fact, our two families may be more closely related than you have hitherto realised.'

'In what way?'

'Your father was the Fifth Earl of Chester, was he not? Hugh de Kevelioc?'

'Obviously he was, else I would not be the sixth earl in the line. What point are you making?'

'Your father had a sister — an older sister called Adele?'

'So I believe, although we never met because she was illegitimate. She would have been my aunt, but I know not what happened to her.'

'I do,' Hugh replied. 'I visited her tomb not so many months ago.'

'And why would you do that?'

'Because she was my mother. We are cousins, it would seem.'

Ranulf let out a whoop of pleasure, then held out his hand for Hugh to shake it warmly. 'I knew there was some bond between us,' he enthused. 'I felt it when we were first introduced. How long have you known?'

'A few years. My father disclosed it when I mentioned that I had been travelling with you through the king's former lands. They were married during the same ceremony that saw your father married to Bertrade de Montfort, while in the same ceremony Amicia of Leicester was betrothed to the young Simon de Montfort. If she is still in life, she will no doubt be our hostess in that splendid house up ahead that I hope is Évreux, since it will mark the end of our long journey.'

It was indeed the Évreux Château at the end of the long drive lined with acacia bushes that sent out a delicate perfume as their flowering season came to an end. But their elation turned to frustration when advised by the estate steward that the entire family could be found a further day's ride towards Paris, on their other estate of Montfort-l'Amaury that was more favoured by the current head of the family, Simon. Hugh calculated that he would be the son of the previous Simon who had married Amicia de Beaumont.

After a comfortable overnight stay, and the reassuring news that the de Montforts were playing host to an important English noble who had found favour with King Philip, Hugh and Ranulf set out with high hopes along the winding track that led predominantly through forests. As the sun was beginning to set, they came in sight of a well fortified castle. Introducing themselves to the guard on the heavy front gates as emissaries from King John of England on their way to Paris, they were admitted to the Great Hall and served with ale, bread and cheese while they waited.

'Was John of England so disappointed with my efforts to secure a peace treaty that he sent others to do a better job?' demanded a loud voice in the doorway. In walked a tall man who moved with the easy confidence of a skilled and experienced warrior. His grey hair was grizzled, but there were wrinkles around the eyes that betrayed a ready sense of humour. Ranulf was about to introduce himself and Hugh when the man spoke again, indicating the smaller man of approximately the same age who was a few paces behind him.

'Forgive my manners,' the first man said, 'and allow me to introduce your host, Simon de Montfort, almost the last of that name, although there are two sons, one of whom is also called Simon, just to confuse the servants.'

Ranulf gave a courtly bow, raised his eyebrows and asked, 'My cousin of sorts, as I calculate?'

De Montfort looked him up and down, and without indicating either approval or disapproval he replied, 'By what process?'

'Your aunt was named Bertrade, and she married into an English family?'

'So they say, but we heard nothing more of her.'

'Her husband was the Fifth Earl of Chester. I am the sixth.'

'So my aunt was your mother?'

'Precisely so. That makes us second cousins by virtue of a common grandfather.'

'Then you are doubly welcome in this house, both as distant family, and — so the steward informs me — as ambassadors of King John on your way to Paris.'

'We are indeed sent by King John,' Ranulf confirmed, 'but our mission is to speak privately with the man standing next you to, if he be William Marshal.'

'I am he,' Marshal replied gruffly, 'so what is your business? And who is the man with you? By his bearing, he is a soldier — is he your bodyguard?'

'I am,' Hugh confirmed. 'And I am a little disappointed that you do not remember me from our final days in Rouen.'

'I have chosen to put that miserable time behind me,' Marshal growled, 'and I was not there long. John sent me to Paris, there to negotiate peace terms, and I may say that I found a readier welcome there than I ever enjoyed at John's Court.'

'That I can well believe,' Ranulf replied diplomatically, 'but we are sent by John to invite you back to Westminster.'

Marshal swore quietly.

De Montfort smiled. 'I will leave you to discuss what is no doubt private business, while I give orders for extra places to be set for supper. As my cousin — however distant — will you and your companion accept my hospitality?'

'With the greatest of pleasure and gratitude,' Ranulf said. 'If we might be shown to our chambers, we need to discard these riding garments and wash.'

An hour later Hugh, Ranulf and Marshal sat in the glasshouse in which tomato plants were climbing towards the dying rays of the sun. Marshal was clearly both suspicious of John's motives for seeking his return to England, and reluctant to even consider it, but Ranulf was hesitant to deliver the king's threat regarding the forfeiture of his estates.

'How fares England under that rash lunatic?' Marshal demanded bluntly.

Ranulf gave an open-armed gesture. 'As you would expect. He seems bent upon retrieving his possessions on this side of the Channel, and has embarked upon a policy of taxation to raise the necessary finance for mercenaries.'

'Why does he need mercenaries, when England possesses some of the finest warriors in the world?' Marshal challenged.

'These are the same knights who John is taxing. They express reluctance to risk their heads in battle, given John's shortcomings as a military leader, and he reacts with the demand that if they will not fight in person, then they must pay for the hiring of those that will fight in their stead. The imposition of taxes makes them even more reluctant to show loyalty, and so the matter descends into a downward spiral of mutual distrust.'

'And what of the Council of which I am presumably still a member?' Marshal asked.

Hugh shook his head. 'It has not met for some time, for precisely the same reasons that Ranulf just explained. This leaves John to impose his will without the benefit of wiser counsellors — not that he paid any heed to them anyway.'

'And what of Archbishop Walter?' was Marshal's next question. 'He was ever able to calm John sufficiently to at least consider more moderate strategies, and more in keeping with his position as nominal head of the Church.'

'Hubert Walter is dead,' Ranulf said.

Marshal gave a groan and lowered his head, before looking up and enquiring, 'And who is his replacement?'

'That's another problem,' Hugh replied with a frown. 'It seems that John is insisting on his own nominee — the current

Bishop of Norwich — but the monks of the Canterbury Chapter want their own sub-prior, a man named Reginald.'

'The Bishop of Norwich is a man called de Gray, is he not?' Marshal asked, and when Ranulf nodded in confirmation, he spat into the earth. 'He has loaned large sums of money to John over the years, and has proven himself adept at wringing money out of others in John's cause. He is about as close to God as my horse.' It fell awkwardly silent for a moment, and the conflict was evident in Marshal's face as he went on, 'Does John give any indication that he will accept my advice, should I return?'

'He did not say,' Hugh conceded, then decided that perhaps they should play their strongest card. 'But he *did* threaten to confiscate your estates if you do not.'

Marshal gave a hollow laugh. 'They are my wife's estates. I came into this world with next to nothing, as my enemies constantly remind anyone who will listen, and I may well depart this world with nothing, so the loss of my estates is no threat. I have effectively abandoned my wife, since it is my intention to become a Knight of the Temple and embark on a Holy Crusade, and the knights are not allowed wives.'

'Crusade?' Hugh echoed. 'Have the Infidels once again closed Jerusalem to Christian pilgrims?'

Marshal shook his head. 'Not that I have heard. The Crusade to which I refer has been ordered by Pope Innocent, against a group of heretics in the Languedoc, which is to the south of here. Our host, Lord Simon, has taken the Holy Cross, and will ride out against the Cathars as soon as his son, also named Simon, can sit upright. He is at present merely a babe in arms, although his older brother Amaury shows promise as a man at arms, following his training by me. That is my primary reason for declining John's request for my return. Tell him that I now serve God, rather than having to watch while mammon consumes the land of my birth.'

'Will you not return even for the sake of England?' Ranulf asked in a final effort to win him round.

'England deserves John, unless it comes to its senses,' said Marshal. 'I am not the man to try to turn the head of the Devil while I can ride forward under God's banner. Come back and find me when England is in its final death throes and I might reconsider. For the time being, you are on your own.'

# X

Hugh and Ranulf were hardly surprised by John's reaction to the news they had to impart on their return to Westminster, but that did not make it any easier to bear. As John's rage reached the point at which it seemed that he might expire from the sheer effort of ranting, swearing, jumping up and down and kicking items of furniture, they began to fear for their own lives.

'What did you do to prevail upon the traitor to return?' he bellowed.

'We delivered your threat to dispossess him of all his estates, sire,' Ranulf confirmed, in as calm a tone as he could manage.

'*And?*' John demanded. 'What was his response?'

Sensing that silence was worse than the truth at this precise moment, Hugh added, 'That the estates are his wife's, sire.'

'Not for a single day longer!' John screamed. 'Lose no time in entering Pembroke with as many men as you can muster, and tell the whore that she is now destitute, and that her arrogant husband is under attainder for treason if he ever again sets one foot on English soil. Do it, and do it *now*! Be gone, before I change my mind regarding *your* loyalties!'

Outside the chamber they heaved sighs of relief, then turned to look at each other.

'Do we do what he demands?' Hugh asked.

'Will we pay with our heads if we don't?' Ranulf replied with his arms spread wide in a gesture of helplessness.

Hugh gave a responding shrug and asked about the best route to take to Pembroke. 'I've never been any closer to Wales than my own estate in Flint,' he admitted.

Ranulf nodded. 'Then allow me to be your guide. Then we might journey back to Cheshire by way of the Welsh Marches. By this means we can visit our families, and hopefully you can give Geoffrey the glad tidings regarding his courtly education on the Chester estate.'

Within the week, they had travelled the full extent of the West Country and found themselves on the southern outskirts of Hereford. There they presented themselves to the castellan of the mighty castle that had been built there as part of England's Marcher defences against the independent Principality of Wales, now under the rule of King Llywelyn mab Iorwerth, whose wife was John's illegitimate daughter Joan.

They were joined at supper by the local Bishop of Hereford, Giles de Braose, and his Archdeacon Walter FitzWalter, at least one of whom had a particular reason for seeking them out.

'I believe that you were in service to the king when my brother William, Lord of Gower, was in charge of the custody of the Prince Arthur at Falaise?' Bishop Giles asked.

'William de Braose?' Hugh said, and when the bishop nodded, he added, 'Indeed. I hadn't made the connection, but he and I shared the responsibilities. I remember him fondly.'

'It's a pity that King John doesn't,' the bishop replied with a scowl, 'although from what I hear of his reputation for honour, truth and integrity, that's hardly surprising. A man who fails to open his heart to God will often fall into the sins of perjury and disloyalty.'

'King John has repaid your brother poorly for his services?' Ranulf asked, and the bishop nodded. 'At first all was sweetness and light. William was awarded several additional estates, including one half a day's ride from here, at Grosmont. Then John began to demand large sums of money in return, as if William had purchased the estates, rather than being gifted them. The sums involved are well beyond the ability of my brother — or indeed *any* baron — to pay, and the king has already distrained on his existing estates in Sussex and Devon. William fears that John will continue his persecution, and seek to have him taken up on treason charges. I will be honest with you and admit that part of my reason for joining you this evening is to establish whether or not you have been sent with that mission. If so, you must know that William has fled to Ireland.'

Hugh laughed. 'With respect, Bishop, that suggestion is quite ludicrous. Our mission lies further west, in Pembroke, and we were privy to no accusation against your brother. I would find it hard to believe that he could ever be guilty of treason, so what possible grounds can John have for such a vile accusation?'

'You and he were jointly responsible for the safe custody of Prince Arthur, you say?' the bishop asked.

'Indeed we were.'

'And John has not, since that time, sought to accuse you of being responsible for Arthur's death?'

'Most certainly not,' Hugh insisted indignantly, 'and I can advise you privily that Arthur left the safety of Falaise and was transferred to Rouen shortly after your brother's return to England on a mission for King John himself. If anything untoward had happened to Arthur during his last days at Falaise, it would have been my head on the block. But I am honesty-bound to advise you that my men had been withdrawn from guard duties by the time that the word was spread abroad that Arthur had died from neglect in his cell. But as I say, he was in robust health when transferred to Rouen.'

'So is he still alive?' asked the archdeacon, who had so far remained silent.

Hugh and Ranulf exchanged uneasy glances, and it was Ranulf who replied.

'We can confirm that he is now dead,' he announced solemnly, 'although I am not at liberty to disclose how, since the lives of two of my men depend upon it.'

'But at least you could, if called upon, testify to the world that his death was in no way attributable to my brother's negligence?' the bishop asked eagerly.

Hugh nodded. 'Although you must appreciate that we are both in the king's service, and must therefore be very circumspect in our public utterances.'

Both the clerics nodded, and the archdeacon silently made the sign of the cross.

'God bless you both for your candour this far. My brother will be interested to learn of one more attempt by the king to shift the blame for his misdeeds onto the heads of the innocent.'

'Your brother?' Ranulf asked.

Archdeacon FitzWalter raised an eyebrow towards Hugh. 'Robert FitzWalter, Constable of Baynard's Castle? He was also in the royal service in your day, and has now been falsely accused of cowardice, along with Saer de Quincy, for surrendering the fortress of Vaudreuil to Philip of France. You will recall that, I imagine?'

'I most certainly do,' Hugh confirmed. 'It proved crucial to our defence of Normandy, and could be said to have been the beginning of the end of John's fortunes over there. You are about to tell me that your brother and his companion were falsely accused of cowardice?'

FitzWalter gave a grunt of disapproval. 'Can it be cowardice to obey a king's command?'

The stunned silence that followed was broken by Ranulf.

'You are telling us that the king himself ordered the surrender?'

'Indeed he did,' the archdeacon confirmed with a downturned mouth. 'The two men pleaded with John to hold his ground and allow them to defend the castle, but John was insistent, threatening them both with treason if they disobeyed him. Even as a man of God I can appreciate what a blunder that must have been in strategic terms, and when it threatened to make a mockery of John's military judgment, he turned on Robert and Saer and accused them of cowardice. The two men were held to ransom by King Philip of France, and it almost ruined their estates when John refused to contribute a penny towards their release. My brother is still incensed by that abandonment, not to mention the slur on his reputation. He would be only too delighted to learn ought regarding the death of Arthur that would demonstrate to the world what a consummate liar John can be when his image is at stake.'

'What of de Quincy?' Hugh asked. 'Is he of similar mind?'

'I have not heard of him for some time,' FitzWalter replied. 'He is married to Margaret, sister of Robert de Beaumont of Leicester, and currently rides under his banner. There is a further connection with the de Braose family there, of course, since Leicester is married to Loretta de Braose, the niece of the lord bishop here.'

'To continue this somewhat tangled tale of interconnected families,' Bishop de Braose added, 'my niece and Robert of Leicester are childless, and Robert is in poor health at present. He has bequeathed the Leicester estates to his two sisters, one of whom is Amicia, wife of Simon de Montfort of France. The other is Margaret, so de Quincy can expect to inherit some of the Leicester estates in the Midlands.'

Hugh shook his head, as if seeking to clear it of cobwebs. 'It never ceases to amaze me how the leading families of England are so closely connected. If you scratch the surface of one, five others emerge underneath. But may de Quincy be reasonably expected to harbour the same feelings of betrayal by John that your brother Robert FitzWalter holds in his heart?'

'I would imagine so, if he be half a man,' the archdeacon replied. 'And neither of them is likely to take kindly to your progress into Wales, given the current state of unrest within England. There are rumours that King John is seeking an alliance with Llewelyn of Wales, in order to acquire warriors who will assist him to retake Normandy. Particularly for those of us who exist here on the borders of that nation, that is unsettling news. We would rather that Llewelyn remain where he is.'

'I can assure you that we are not sent to parley with the Welsh king,' Ranulf replied.

'Then what is your reason for coming so far west?' the bishop asked.

Ranulf and Hugh exchanged a look, and when Ranulf nodded, Hugh began to explain. 'King John is displeased with the refusal of William Marshal to return to England, and has ordered that his wife be advised that because of this refusal, she is to lose her Pembroke estate. We are sent with that message.'

The bishop sighed. 'I almost feel that I should be offering you fine men absolutions for your sins. You clearly ride in the Devil's vanguard, and I would simply ask that you examine your consciences before you proceed much further.'

'Why do I feel soiled merely by being in the royal service?' Hugh asked as they rode south-west along the narrow track through the Brecon Hills that would take them to Pembroke.

'I feel like washing my hands every time I even *think* of that,' Ranulf complained, 'and at least your service is the more honourable military one. I'm one of his ambassadors, and I took to heart what the bishop said about working for the Devil.'

'If we're not careful, we'll be as reviled as John himself seems to be in some quarters,' Hugh added. 'Doors will be slammed in our faces before we even reach them to announce our business. Here we are, on the final leg of a long journey to advise a woman with a multitude of children that she's about to be thrown off her lands.'

They need not have concerned themselves unduly on that score. When they presented themselves to the steward of Pembroke Castle, they were advised that the countess had taken herself across the sea to her estates in Ireland, where she hoped to be reunited with her husband. 'She scorns to land again in England, given the rude reports he has received regarding King John's regard for her husband's negotiations with the French king. You are here on the king's business?'

'We are,' Ranulf confirmed as Hugh looked down at his riding boots in embarrassment, 'but I fear that our commission will not be to your liking. It is to the effect that the countess Isabel is longer infeft of Pembroke. The king has taken it back into his possession.'

'In truth, it was never *in* his possession,' the steward remarked with a sour expression. 'The Earldom of Pembroke came to the Lady Isabel's husband only a few years ago, and I was proud to serve her father, Earl Richard de Clare, before then, and before she married that adventurer from across the sea. So King John may seize the estate if he will, but it was never his by lawful right. It will go ill with the mistress's cousin of sorts, Richard de Clare, who is the Earl of Hertford and Earl of Gloucester by marriage, although John will not recognise that marriage, on account of his apprehension that Earl Richard will thereby become too powerful. However, it will be glad tidings for the King of Wales.'

'And why might that be?' Ranulf asked.

'Because he has long sought to expand his kingdom with the lands here in Pembroke, and also at Chepstow, to the east of here and beside the channel that leads to Bristol. If he were to overrun the latter, he would of course be close on the English border, so if King John is minded to seize the Chepstow estate as well, he would be well advised to see to its defences, as well as those here in Pembroke.'

'And how do you know what is in the mind of the King of Wales?' Ranulf demanded.

He was met with a haughty glare from the steward. 'Because, unlike some that I could mention, I keep up a regular communication with my neighbours,' he replied. 'Llywelyn of Wales speaks excellent English, and has more than once been an honoured guest here, while my mistress and William Marshal have been entertained several times at his palace in Aber Garth Celyn.'

'So, it is your belief that if your earl and countess are no longer seized of this estate, King Llywelyn will move in?' asked Hugh.

The steward nodded. 'You might wish to advise His Majesty of that possibility.'

'Advise him or *warn* him?' Hugh asked.

The steward shrugged. 'I can only reply that we have, in recent years, received greater kindness and courtesy from the

Welsh king than we have ever experienced at the hands of his English neighbour. Now, do you wish to be accommodated overnight?'

'So where to now?' Hugh asked as they trotted out of Pembroke Castle the following morning.

'I was giving that some thought last night when I couldn't sleep,' Ranulf replied.

'Your conscience?'

'Your snoring. And yes, you *do*. How does Edwina put up with it?'

'She's never mentioned it. Perhaps she's deaf. But where do you think we should go next?'

'Clearly,' Ranulf replied, 'we've done what John asked of us. Now let's do something he didn't order.'

'Such as?'

'Well, from what I heard from our surly host yesterday, there is a potential threat from Wales. Some time ago, John asked me to check on the current state of our Marcher estates, and I did — although he never bothered asking for my report after he reacted so angrily to the presumption of the monks of Canterbury in putting up one of their own as archbishop. So I suggest that we head back through Hereford into Gloucestershire, then north through Worcestershire and Staffordshire into my own estates.'

'Can we call into Repton on our way north?' Hugh asked. 'I'd like to visit my brother Robert, who I haven't seen for some years.'

Ranulf nodded. 'Then into Flint, where you can give Geoffrey the glad tidings that he'll be spending some time with *his* Uncle Ranulf.'

Their progress through the earldoms of the West Midlands only served to add to their unease at being labelled emissaries of King John. The reactions to them in Gloucester, Worcester, Stafford and Leicester varied from mildly suspicious to downright hostile, and in each case the cause of the anti-royal sentiment seemed to be centred around John's constant demands for taxes. He'd also threatened to distrain on estates from which the money was not forthcoming, had imposed fines for suspected and largely illusory malfeasances, and had promoted to high offices of State personal favourites drawn from his wife's Poitevin relatives.

'At least we shall be guaranteed a warm welcome at this next estate,' Hugh said as they trotted along the track to the side of the woodland that they'd been following ever since leaving the village of Ashby. The roof of Repton Manor House became clearer and clearer, with the spire of the priory church a mile or so behind it. Once they had passed through the gap in the yew hedge that marked the entrance to the estate, Hugh raised himself in his stirrups and gave a loud, 'Halloo!'

From the doorway of the manor house came a familiar figure, much heavier than he had been when Hugh had last seen him. His mop of hair, once as black as any crow's, was now patched with grey, but there was no mistaking Robert.

Hugh dismounted, and they embraced. Then Hugh turned to where Ranulf was standing awkwardly to the side and effected the introductions.

'We are in urgent need of ale, bread, and some of that delicious local cheese,' he told Robert.

'You must have smelt it on the table, for we have a guest. Your arrival could not be better timed, since you may be called upon to lay siege to Nottingham Castle yet again.'

# XI

The man already seated at the table in the Hall was introduced to the new arrivals as Roger de Montbegon, Baron of Hornby.

'Forgive me,' Hugh said after being introduced, 'but where exactly *is* Hornby?'

'Lancashire,' Roger replied. 'It is hard by Lancaster, if you have heard of it. I am also infeft of estates in Lincolnshire and Yorkshire, but it is a dispute regarding my holdings in your neighbouring county of Nottinghamshire that bring me here.'

'And why here?' Hugh demanded, annoyed that his happy homecoming was being blighted by a request for assistance from this weak-chinned and somewhat ingratiating intruder.

'Lord Robert here has an enduring reputation as a man who led an army of unarmed peasants against the all-powerful sheriff who was holding Nottingham Castle against King Richard.'

'If you are referring to the men of the Shire Wood,' Hugh replied testily, 'then you should know that they were neither peasants nor unarmed. They were all freemen who had been dispossessed by the sheriff at that time, a rat called de Wendenal who died following the siege of Nottingham Castle by the forces of King Richard, among which I was proud to be a man at arms. The Shire Wood men were of great service when, with their bows, they cleared the battlements of the men who were denying us entry.'

'So you *and* your brother here were involved in the siege?'

'That is correct, but why have you come here to enquire?' Hugh demanded.

'I wish you to repeat that feat, this time against Sheriff Philip Marc.'

'Commit treason, you mean?' Hugh asked coldly. 'Please explain — *very* carefully — why I should even consider doing that, given that Sir Ranulf and I are both in the king's service.'

'So was I, *once*,' de Montbegon replied with a sneer that made him resemble a ferret.

'You are no longer?' Ranulf asked. 'Why might that be?'

'Because of his ungrateful treatment of me, in instructing the sheriff that I may not take seisin of my estates at Clayworth, Oswaldbeck and North Wheatley, all of which lie in the east of the adjacent county. After the manner in which I served him during the years in which he was seeking to bring peace to the realm while his brother Richard was in foreign parts, I deserve better.'

It fell silent for a moment, both Robert and Ranulf waiting to see if Hugh would draw the obvious inference. He did.

'Let me see if I have this correct,' he replied calmly and coldly. 'While King Richard was embarked upon a Crusade to reclaim the Holy Land for Christian pilgrims, under the banner of the Pope, and during his subsequent lengthy imprisonment, you were one of those who sought to assist John in undermining the authority of the true king. Is that what you are telling us?'

'That is the case, yes.'

'And you are of the belief that John has not rewarded you sufficiently for your efforts?'

'That is also correct. And I have the support of many like myself in the north who are on the point of rebellion due to the king's constant demand for money, and the seizure of estates without lawful cause. If you assist me in taking the local sheriff prisoner, we may use him as a hostage in order to persuade King John to redress our grievances.'

'You may leave now, before I throw you out on your head!' Hugh replied as the colour rose in his cheeks.

Ranulf placed a hand on Hugh's sleeve. 'What my companion means,' he said, 'is that you may leave here alive only when you have named those who you claim are to be found north of here, planning a rebellion.'

The colour drained from de Montbegon's face as he looked first at Hugh, then back to Ranulf. 'You would have me betray my friends?'

'Why not?' Hugh replied with a sneer. 'You were seeking to betray your king.'

By the time that de Montbegon was allowed to leave, Hugh and Ranulf had a list of all those who were contemplating some sort of uprising against the throne, and were discussing how best to use it.

'We could ride back to Westminster and deliver the list to John,' Hugh suggested, but Ranulf shook his head.

'We would be relying on the word of a man who came here seeking your assistance for personal gain. His concern was not for the fate of the realm, nor even to expose the malfeasance of one public officer. Would you risk your life on the word of such a man? If we were to seek an audience with John, and present him with a list of those alleged to be plotting against him, how do you think he would be likely to react?'

'Very angrily,' Hugh conceded. 'And he would no doubt demand proof of such a serious allegation — that there is an uprising in the offing.'

'Precisely,' Ranulf nodded. 'How much better would it be, both for John *and* ourselves, if we were able to advise him that we had spoken to each of these barons in turn, and confirmed for ourselves that they are planning to tilt against the throne?'

'But we can hardly present ourselves at each of their doors, enquiring politely in our capacities as royal emissaries whether or not it is true that they are contemplating an act of treason.'

'Of course not,' Ranulf said knowingly, 'which is why, when we come calling, we pretend that we too are disenchanted with John's cruel and lawless actions, and that we would wish to join the rebellion.'

'That would not be too far from the truth,' Hugh reminded him, 'bearing in mind our original mission into Pembroke, and what we learned in Hereford. But it is surely in the nation's best interests, at this time, that we support John and do our utmost to persuade him into more just and honourable policies.'

'And we do that by demonstrating beyond doubt that we are to be trusted, and can deliver his enemies into his hands,' Ranulf insisted. 'Then perhaps he will listen to us when we advise him of the road he must travel in order to secure loyalty from *all* the leading barons, and not just those fools from Poitou who surround his throne.'

Hugh glanced back down at the list, then frowned. 'We will need to travel far and wide, to judge by these names. I had hoped to spend some time back at home with my family.'

'And so you shall,' Ranulf reassured him. 'You are not the only one who yearns to be back in the comfort of his own estate, surrounded by loved ones. Let us take two weeks to refresh ourselves, then bring Geoffrey over to Chester to reside with my family and learn the manners of the Court.'

'He has yet to complete his training in arms,' Hugh objected.

Ranulf offered to allow Geoffrey to continue weapons training as part of the garrison inside Chester Castle. 'Roger de

Lacy is a stern taskmaster, and will ensure that your boy lacks for nothing in preparing him to become a sturdy man at arms. He may reside within Chester Castle for a month at a time, then spend the next month back in my manor house, which as you know is a mere stroll down the street from the castle.'

'I have yet to convince his mother,' Hugh grimaced.

Ranulf laughed as he clapped him on the shoulder. 'Are you a man or a mouse, Hugh? You have faced armed men on the field of battle, you once rescued two queens from a shipwreck, and you defended Montreuil almost single-handed. Yet you quail before the scorn of a *woman*?'

'Not just *any* woman, my friend,' Hugh replied. 'And you are correct in your assessment of my greatest weakness. I fear her wrath more than any armed opponent.'

'It's come to a sorry day when you pay more regard to the urgings of the Earl of Chester than you do to the immediate interests of the future Earl of Flint!' Edwina fumed as she stood, hand on hips, in her usual defiant stance.

The object of their argument, fifteen-year-old Geoffrey, sat silently watching and hoping that his father would win. After all, while life on the Flint estate was pleasant enough, it had its limitations — particularly regarding the charms of what few local girls were available. As for military training, which he was more interested in, it would be nice to learn from a current man at arms rather than his father who, so far as he could gather, had not wielded a sword in aggression for many years.

'It *is* in Geoffrey's immediate interests to learn how to be a courtier,' Hugh insisted as he weathered the opening blast. 'He will never progress in the royal service simply as a man at arms — he needs to learn courtly manners, and his French must improve if he is to compete for royal favour with those idle fools from Poitou.'

'And where have all those fine achievements taken *you*?' Edwina challenged him. 'You are never at home for more than one week at a time, and you travel the length of the nation, getting saddle sores in the name of a king who is so unpopular that even some of our tenant farmers have taken to calling him "dead nettle". What did you ever gain from serving two kings like a lapdog at its master's feet?'

'I gained *you*, for one thing,' Hugh replied with a triumphant smirk. 'And I would not have been confirmed in this estate without the royal favour I enjoyed at the time.'

Edwina snorted. 'You gained this estate by marrying me, and it was easier for King Richard to confirm you in it than it was to consider some other worthy claimant, particularly since you had recently helped him retake Nottingham Castle.'

'Precisely!' Hugh grinned in triumph. 'It was my very wise decision to marry a queen's lady that gained me this estate. And *she* only became a queen's lady in the first place — and therefore suitable for marriage to a lord — because of her courtly ways. Or would you prefer that Geoffrey remain a landlord farmer — a journeyman grower of sheep and vegetables?'

'Of course not!' Edwina protested. 'It's just that he's too young yet to be exposed to the wiles of the Court, which I recall only too well myself, remember. When I oppose Geoffrey's proposed departure from here, I speak as a former lady at Court.'

'No, you speak as a mother,' Hugh argued. 'And have you taken the time to enquire of our son what *he* wishes to do? Or is his happiness of no importance to you?'

It fell silent, and Geoffrey was not sure whether or not he was being invited to speak until his father turned to him with raised eyebrows.

'If you genuinely wish to know what I desire,' he offered timidly, 'then it is to progress in life as the Earl of Flint one day. The best way to achieve that, as I see it, is to become a valued member of the household of the adjoining, and much more influential, Earl of Chester. And I'm tired of testing my sword on bags filled with sand, and my lance on targets hanging from trees in the home meadow.'

'See?' Hugh grinned at Edwina. 'Even the boy himself can see the sense of what Ranulf and I are proposing.'

'You wish to leave your mother — and all this — behind?' Edwina asked, seemingly crestfallen.

Geoffrey stepped across to place his arm lovingly around her shoulders. 'I will only be on the adjoining estate, Mother,' he reminded her. 'There will be ample opportunity for me to make journeys back to my real home.'

'I can see that I am overborne by the two men in my life,' Edwina conceded grumpily. 'At least little Edith still wishes to remain with the one who gave her birth.' Then she punched Geoffrey lightly on his tunic shoulder. 'Mind that you visit here more often than your father.'

Four days later Geoffrey rode out proudly alongside his father, dressed in his best battle array. The servants lined up to wish him farewell, several of the serving girls suppressing tears as they watched the two horses with their riders disappear down the estate track and through its front entrance.

Hugh and Ranulf delivered Geoffrey into the custody of Roger de Lacy, not without some misgivings on Hugh's part when the constable assured him that although he had been given a boy, he would return him as a man. Afterwards, the king's emissaries made their way towards the Cheshire Manor House on the town side of the river bridge that Ranulf had constructed for his own convenience.

'So where to first?' Hugh asked.

Ranulf frowned. 'We have a choice, it would seem, since the estates we must visit are so widely spread, although in the main they are north of here. I suggest that we begin in Malton, which I'm advised is somewhere north of York. That is where Eustace de Vesci has his estate, and from him we can no doubt obtain an introduction to his kinsman Robert de Ros, whose estate is a little north of that. Then we can work our way south through the realm until we are once again back in the Midland counties.'

'I will of course be guided by you,' Hugh agreed, 'but it is to be hoped that the money given to us for our journey to Pembroke does not run out by the time we have completed such a daunting round trip of the nation.'

'If it does, we merely have any debts that we incur remitted to the Treasury,' Ranulf said. 'We will, after all, be working to preserve the throne for our paymaster.'

It took them several weeks to follow the main North Road to York, and thereafter the country tracks that wound over moorlands and barren heath broken only by isolated castles and defence towers. They finally found sanctuary in two castles owned by leading northern barons who were only too content to air their grievances to the two eager men who claimed to be former emissaries of King John.

Hugh and Ranulf learned, without any effort on their part, that there was a rapidly growing undercurrent of discontent that was uniting some of the leading barons in the land in a plan to confront King John en masse and demand a change of policy. No-one to whom they spoke was prepared to raise men at arms to answer the recent call for an army to march into Poitou as an overture to the retaking of Normandy, nor was anyone intending to pay the latest scutage tax demanded by the king. Instead, it had been agreed that once John attempted to take action against the first of those who had joined the coalition of the disgruntled, they would all march to London as one force. There they had been promised support and additional men at arms by Robert FitzWalter, who not only held estates at Great Dunmow in Essex, but was also the Constable of Baynard's Castle, conveniently located close to the mighty Tower of London that housed much of King John's weaponry during peacetime.

The resentment that was building against John's policies was even more in evidence when Hugh and Ranulf finally headed south through Thirsk and Lincolnshire. They were welcomed onto the estates of William de Mowbray, who was still engaged in a lengthy court battle regarding the estate of Cottingham, just north of the River Humber. It had been awarded to the Mowbray family after its previous owner Robert de Stuteville had forfeited it for treason, but Robert's son William had brought an action for its recovery in the King's Court, and had bribed John with two thousand marks to ensure that it ended in a compromise favourable to de Stuteville. De Mowbray had been left with an enormous bill for legal fees that he was struggling to pay off.

There were even more obvious grievances to be aired when Ranulf and Hugh found themselves as the guests of Saer de Quincy on his Northamptonshire estate of Brackley. De Quincy had been, along with Robert FitzWalter, one of the joint castellans of Vaudreuil who had been ordered by John to surrender it to the forces of Philip of France, and then accused of cowardice in its surrender. Not even his recent elevation to the Earldom of Winchester had served to douse de Quincy's burning resentment of this slight on his reputation. The flames had been further fanned by John's obstinacy in failing to recognise his title to the Leicestershire estate of Mountsorrel, part of the inheritance of his wife Margaret when Earl Robert de Beaumont had recently died without heirs.

The name of Robert FitzWalter was also much mentioned when Hugh and Ranulf were entertained on the Rutland estate of William d'Albini at Belvoir. D'Albini was FitzWalter's first cousin, and shared with him a growing disenchantment with John's arbitrary and oppressive policies. D'Albini was also the uncle of Robert de Ros, who Hugh and Ranulf had already visited on his North Yorkshire estate of Helmsley during their tour of the nation. It was rapidly becoming clear that the growing unrest among the barons was rooted as much in family loyalties as it was in any personal antipathy to the king.

A family loyalty that once again pointed to Robert FitzWalter being the spider at the centre of the web when they arrived finally at Dunmow, in Essex, whose lord was Geoffrey de Mandeville, formerly married to FitzWalter's daughter Maud. When Maud had died, de Mandeville had taken as his second wife Isabella of Gloucester, the former wife of King John, and the former Queen of England. In her own right she was the very wealthy heiress of the Gloucester estates, and John had seized the opportunity, as king rather than as a former spouse, to demand twenty thousand marks from de Mandeville in order to take up the inheritance, which was to revert to the Crown in the event of non-payment by quarterly instalments. Geoffrey was unlikely to be able to make even the first payment, and was seething with rage at the king's greed.

Before finally setting their mounts' noses in the direction of London, Ranulf and Hugh were able to add other names to the rapidly growing list of those who only required some leadership before they could unite in a powerful uprising against John. Among the names supplied by recent hosts were Henry de Bohun, Earl of Hertford — who was in acrimonious dispute with John's half-brother the Earl of Salisbury over the lordship of Trowbridge in Wiltshire — and the powerful and wealthy Richard de Clare, the last in a line of nobles who had once owned half of England. He was connected by family ties to Geoffrey de Mandeville in that de Clare's wife Amicia was the sister of de Mandeville's wife Isabel.

Ranulf and Hugh decided to take time to consider their best way forward with all the potentially devastating information in their possession. They sat at a rustic table outside an alehouse in Barnet, basking in the warm midday sun and confident that the hustle and bustle of street activity would mask their conversation from any eavesdropper.

'If we take this list to John immediately,' Hugh suggested, 'we can not only prove our ongoing worth to him, but also assure him of our ongoing loyalty before the storm breaks.'

'What makes you think that a storm *will* break?' Ranulf asked cautiously.

'Clearly, the barons we have spoken to personally are on the point of rebellion, such is their resentment of their treatment at John's hands,' Hugh replied.

'That is certainly the impression that they gave to each of us. But should we repeat those words to the king, and should he challenge those responsible for uttering them, they will simply deny it. If the ten or so who we would be accusing of treasonous thoughts all deny having uttered the words that we report, who do you think John will believe? The two of us, or the ten of them? And always keep in mind John's vanity — he is likely to want to believe that all his subjects love and revere him, and will not take kindly to any suggestion to the contrary.'

'Then what shall we do with the information in our possession?' Hugh asked.

'We beard the wolf in his lair,' Ranulf announced. 'We visit Robert FitzWalter and pretend that after speaking with all those discontented with John's rule, we wish to have our names added to the list of those who will stand against him when the battle horn is blown.'

'Will he believe us, think you?'

'There's only one way to find out. Finish that ale and let's retrieve our horses from the stable.'

# XII

The strategic importance of Baynard's Castle was obvious from several miles away, as Ranulf and Hugh guided their mounts down the track alongside the Fleet River. Where it joined the mighty Thames, there was a fortification that could easily be held against an army, and could withstand a siege without difficulty, given the access to the river and the distant sea. It would also be a convenient place from which to escape the royal wrath, the two men agreed, as they noted the presence of a large vessel in the moat that had a river access, and which could bear its passengers downriver to the open ocean and across the Channel.

They'd agreed their ploy in advance. When they were joined in the Great Hall into which they'd been admitted by the steward, and Robert FitzWalter shook their hands in welcome, then took a second, quizzical, look at Hugh, he had his response ready.

'We met at Rouen several years past, before you were sent to defend Vaudreuil in company with Saer de Quincy,' Hugh reminded him.

Robert's face reddened in anger. 'Are you here bringing more allegations from the two-faced king regarding our alleged cowardice?' he demanded.

Hugh smiled. 'Far from it. Would it ease your mind were I to advise you that we lately spoke with de Quincy himself regarding that matter?'

FitzWalter's expression eased somewhat as he asked, 'And did he advise you of the true facts?'

'He said that the order to surrender came from the king, under threat of a treason charge if you disobeyed, and that it was only after the sheer enormity of that tactical error became obvious that he sought to cast the blame on you,' Ranulf told him.

'Then why are you here?' FitzWalter demanded.

Hugh adopted a sympathetic expression as he answered for both of them. 'To confirm the truth of what de Quincy said, because if that be the case, then you have been grievously wronged. We both remain in the royal service, and are anxious in case we are in some way assisting in the maltreatment of good loyal subjects such as yourself.'

FitzWalter gave a bitter laugh as he told them, 'I am not the only one who John has mistreated. He accepted a bribe in order to deprive William de Mowbray of his rightful inheritance, he keeps de Quincy from part of his Leicester lands in the hopes of selling it off, and he's obliged my former son-in-law, and good friend, Geoffrey de Mandeville to pay a ruinous sum in order to inherit the Gloucester estates on his remarriage to the former queen. There are many more such outrages I could list, all of them designed to raise money in order to surround himself with fawning Poitevin favourites who are the only ones prepared to assure him that he has a hope in Hell of reclaiming his estates in Normandy. If you serve him, and if you are possessed of wealth, be prepared to suffer at his hands.'

'As you know, I am possessed of many estates in Cheshire that come with my earldom,' Ranulf replied with a convincing look of concern. 'You say that King John will seek in some way to dispossess me of them in order to enjoy the revenue therefrom?'

'Almost certainly, sooner or later,' FitzWalter all but spat. 'Be prepared for that, and God be with you if you continue to blindly display your loyalty. John will simply take that as a sign of weakness. He prefers to be surrounded by weak men, no doubt because they make him feel strong. I fear for his offspring, because he will subject them to the same disdain and contempt as his father did John and his brothers.'

'It is perhaps as well that there are none,' Hugh replied casually.

FitzWalter's eyebrows rose in surprise. 'Where have you been these past months?' he asked. 'It is the talk of the Court that the queen is with child.'

They took a moment to absorb this latest information before Ranulf picked up the conversation.

'As you rightly surmise, we have been touring the nation at John's request, assessing the mood. I believe that we might trust in your discretion to the extent of advising you that there is a considerable feeling of unrest among the leading barons regarding those matters to which you have already alluded — the Poitevin favourites, the unrealistic hope of regaining Normandy, the forfeiture or withholding of estates. It was our very unpleasant duty to journey to Pembroke, there to advise the former countess that she was no longer infeft as a result of the refusal of her husband William Marshal to return to England. It is feared that in his absence, King Llywelyn of Wales will take the opportunity to expand his kingdom.'

'It is worse even than that,' FitzWalter told them, 'since the Younger Marshal was lately confined to the Tower down the road there. A boy of fifteen who never once displayed an ounce of disloyalty, but is locked away like a common criminal because his father refuses to return in order, no doubt, to be executed. This is how John repays loyalty, gentlemen. Were it not for William Marshal's unswerving devotion to John's brother Richard, and before that their father Henry, then John would not have been in the powerful position he was at his coronation, which he has failed to retain. But tell me — how real is this threat from Wales?'

'We cannot be sure,' Ranulf hedged, 'since we can only go by what we were told by the estate steward in Pembroke. He claims that the Welsh have for a long time looked enviously at the more fertile land of Pembroke, which is kinder on the eye that their slate-hued mountainous wastes in Gwynedd.'

'You obviously know the region well,' FitzWalter observed as he eyed him suspiciously.

Ranulf gave him a bland smile. 'I am a Welsh Marcher Lord, remember. It is my business to be aware of the Welsh territories, and what takes place within them. God forbid that we have to rely on the Marcher Lords further south, in places such as Gloucester, Shrewsbury and Hereford. Speaking of which, we were royally entertained in the bishop's palace in Hereford, where I believe the archdeacon is your brother?'

'That is the case,' FitzWalter replied guardedly. 'What of it?'

'Nothing,' Ranulf replied, 'except that now that John has repossessed Pembroke, if he does not take urgent steps to defend it, the associated estates in Chepstow will come under threat. They are uncomfortably close to Hereford from the point of view of an army of bloodthirsty bowmen, are they not? And the Welsh are not famed for their respect for the Church of Rome and its adherents.'

'I sincerely hope that you will make King John aware of the threat posed by Wales?' FitzWalter asked in alarm.

Ranulf shrugged. 'We hope to be consulted on that matter, but we have so much else to report to him.'

'Regarding the unrest of the barons?'

'That, among other things. But we must now make our way westward to Westminster, in order to demonstrate that loyalty to His Majesty of which you were so dismissive,' Ranulf said as he and Hugh bowed their way out of the hall.

'I think we have him seriously worried,' Hugh said as they remounted.

Ranulf nodded. 'It now remains to be seen how he reacts. I propose that we do not reveal to John the full extent of what we have discovered, but let him learn it for himself. We may perhaps be called upon to suppress a rebellion shortly. Either that or we will be sent back to Baynard's Castle to arrest FitzWalter.'

As they had hoped, John was too preoccupied with two major issues to enquire as to where they had been, and with whom they had spoken, once they confirmed that the Countess of Pembroke had been advised, via her steward, that she was no longer a substantial estate owner in South Wales, but that she was in any case on her Irish estates.

'There was no suggestion that she was stirring up rebellion over there?' John asked nervously.

'The only one she may be consorting with is her husband, since we were advised that he was intending to join her over there,' said Hugh.

'That is all to the good — for him, anyway,' John smirked unpleasantly. 'At least in Ireland he will retain his head. Now, I seek your opinion on this impasse regarding the appointment of a new Archbishop of Canterbury.' When both men looked nonplussed, he went on, 'I wasn't seeking your opinion on a suitable candidate, you fools — simply any information you can supply regarding who might be siding with the Pope in the matter.'

Fortunately they'd taken two days to rest in their grace and favour chambers in the courtyard of Westminster Palace, and had caught up with the major issues that were being discussed around the corridors of power. One of these was the increasing tension regarding a replacement for Hubert Walter, who'd been dead for over a year. This was merely symbolic of a much wider issue, namely the right to control the English clergy.

Ever since the murder of Thomas Becket in 1170, during the reign of his father Henry, John had been careful not to antagonise the Pope in Rome, who exercised considerable temporal power across the Christian nations. When Becket had become a martyr, John had witnessed how his father had been shunned by all the pious monarchs across the Channel. At this precise moment John needed allies, and he was reluctant to alienate powerful nobles in his own kingdom who, unlike him, were easily overawed by tales of hellfire and damnation. He knew that they might feel less loyalty towards him if he fell out with Rome and brought down an interdict on the nation.

Successive Popes, for their part, had taken the subservience of the two subsequent Angevin monarchs as a sign that the authority of Rome was beyond dispute, most notably in the matter of high ecclesiastical appointments. The lack of spiritual grace exhibited by Hubert Walter had been tactfully ignored, given his willingness to obey Papal edicts.

John had nominated John de Gray, Bishop of Norwich, to take his place. De Gray had loaned the king vast sums of money in the past, and had frequently undertaken ambassadorial duties to Paris. But even more important to John was the fact that de Gray had carried the word of mouth order from John that the Castle of Vaudreuil was to be surrendered to Philip of France, a decision for which he had subsequently blamed FitzWalter and de Quincy. A failure to bribe de Gray with the highest ecclesiastical office in the land could prove highly embarrassing to John.

But this appointment was against the wishes of the monks of the cathedral, who were equally insistent on their traditional right to appoint their next spiritual leader. Their preference was for one of their own, the pious Sub-Prior Reginald. They had secretly elected him, then sent him to Rome to be confirmed by Pope Innocent, who was a champion of Church authority over temporal power at any level. Rather than be seen to meekly accept John's choice, regardless of the man's merits, while simultaneously regarding Reginald as a lightweight candidate, the Pope decided to appoint a man of his own choosing, the highly regarded English academic cleric Cardinal Stephen Langton.

Both Hugh and Ranulf were at a loss as to how to answer John's question, but it was Ranulf who attempted a response of sorts.

'I don't suppose it matters to most of our nobles who is the archbishop, sire, so perhaps the Pope's choice is as good as any.'

John's face darkened. 'You miss the important issue, I think. Whoever is chosen becomes the most senior cleric in England. *My* England. Why should I accept the choice of some God mutterer in a fancy gown when the person appointed will have such an important role in the nation's affairs? I have issued an order prohibiting this "Langton" lapdog from entering England, and I wish you both to journey to Canterbury and seize the estates of the see in my name.'

When both men stood in silence, looking uncomfortable, John glared back at each of them in turn. 'You disdain to carry out an order from your king?'

'No, sire,' Ranulf mumbled awkwardly, 'it's just that we are apprehensive of being excommunicated or something.'

'And you believe that to be worse than a hanging?' John retorted ominously.

Ranulf simply replied, 'We shall leave at daybreak tomorrow, sire.'

By the time that Hugh and Ranulf returned from their unpleasant assignment — during which they had been shunned by the monks of Canterbury and denied accommodation in the hospitium of the cathedral's affiliated monastery — word was everywhere that Queen Isabella had given birth to a son at Winchester Castle, to which she had retired for her confinement, away from the unhealthy airs of London. The boy had been named Henry after his grandfather, and the nation was officially rejoicing at the birth of an heir who would continue the Plantagenet dynasty into another generation, bringing peace and certainty to the nation.

That, at least, was the official opinion, and a national holiday was declared, with the usual bacchanalian excesses observed in every town, village and rural hamlet. But when they reached Tonbridge for their final overnight stay before re-entering the capital, Hugh and Ranulf were exposed to another opinion that echoed what they had been hearing during their tour of the rest of the nation.

'Another idle, robbing mouth to feed,' Richard de Clare muttered. Supper in the Great Hall of his castle overlooking the Medway was being served late, because several of his kitchen hands were lying insensibly drunk on the local common after engaging too enthusiastically in the celebrations of the royal birth. 'One possible hope for England was that coxcomb John would die young, without issue. Now it would seem that we shall have to endure another generation of foreign favourites, humiliation in warfare, excessive taxation and unjustified seizure of estates — unless steps are taken to install a true system of justice, in which those who are not in favour at Court this week, and those who have not loaned large sums of money to the Treasury, receive the same treatment as those who have.'

'As I understand the situation,' Hugh replied tentatively as both men recovered from the shock of hearing such openly treasonous words, 'the law that is in place is adequate to provide the sort of justice to which you refer. Indeed, it was my father, during his time as Chief Justice, who made it so. The problem lies in ensuring that the law is administered as it was intended to be, and equally to all.'

'Until someone makes the effort to ensure that this dream becomes reality,' de Clare replied hotly, 'then it will remain precisely that — a dream.' He looked long and hard at each of them in turn before adding, 'You have recently spoken, I think, with Robert FitzWalter?'

'Indeed we have,' Ranulf confirmed uneasily, 'and he expressed a sentiment not unlike yours. But of course he has good grounds for resentment regarding the way the king has dealt with him in the matter of the surrender of Vaudreuil.'

'And you think I have not?' de Clare demanded angrily. 'Have you spoken recently with Geoffrey de Mandeville?'

'We have,' Hugh said, 'and he expressed to us his frustration at being blocked from his wife's share of the Gloucester estates until he paid a ruinous sum of money.'

'And he is not the only one,' de Clare spat. 'Another heiress of those estates is my wife Amicia, and feckless John is throwing every legal obstacle he can in the way of her becoming infeft. The man seems to invent the laws as occasion requires, and always to his ultimate benefit. One day he will learn to his cost that while loyalty must be won slowly over the years, it can be lost due to a single act of treachery or underhanded dealing.' It fell uncomfortably silent, until he went on, 'I shall of course deny having uttered these words, if challenged. But you may wish to decide which side of the barricade you will occupy when the steel is removed from the scabbard.'

Hugh and Ranulf left the next morning, mulling over what they'd been told.

'De Clare had a valid point,' Hugh observed as they crested the slope that led down between the cottages lining the track onto London Bridge. They were on the final mile of their return journey to Westminster, whose towers glowed ahead of them in the midday sunlight.

Ranulf grunted. 'Obviously he did. The question in my mind is whether or not all these disaffected nobles will convert their grievances into action. Where would we be best positioned if they do?'

'We are servants of the Crown, Ranulf,' Hugh reminded him glumly, 'and my service is a direct military one. If the barons rebel, I will be required to defend the king against them.'

'And can you live with your conscience if you do?' Ranulf asked.

Hugh thought for a moment. 'I am sworn to the king's service. What price my honour if I break that oath? And what will become of England if the right to rule it comes not from royal birth but from force of arms?'

'You are probably too honourable to live,' Ranulf grimaced, 'but since you are the only one I can trust with my men at arms, and therefore the security of my estates, I must perforce go along with whatever you decide. I just hope, for our sakes and those of our families, that we prove to be riding the right horse when the race for supremacy begins. *If* it does, and please God that it does not.'

They had anticipated a few days of rest after returning to Westminster, given the festivities surrounding the royal birth and the detailed planning of the baptism ceremony. There was a rumour that this was to be conducted by the Bishop of Norwich, whether or not he was also the Archbishop of Canterbury by that date. But they were summoned to the royal presence on only the second day, and found themselves being harangued by a clearly anxious John.

'You returned to Court two days ago, did you not?'

'Yes, sire,' Ranulf admitted.

'Then why did you not report back to me immediately?' John demanded as the colour rose in his face.

It was Hugh who came up with the excuse. 'There was nothing to report, sire, and we were advised that you were heavily involved in the planning of the baptism ceremony. Congratulations, by the way, on…'

'Spare me the mealy-mouthed platitudes that I have to endure from others!' John barked. 'For your information, the Chamberlain is the one organising the baptism ceremony. When you say that there was nothing to report, you mean that you did nothing?'

'On the contrary, sire,' Ranulf hastened to assure him, 'we served the necessary papers, and the revenues of Canterbury are already being diverted into the Treasury. However, since we had fulfilled our mission without either delay or opposition, we did not feel that you needed to be troubled by our seeking an audience simply to advise that we had achieved what we set out to achieve. Your orders have been carried out.'

'So you have taken to deciding what I should, and should not, be consulted about, is that the case?' John demanded.

Both men shook their heads and waited with bated breath for what that rhetorical question might be heralding.

'As in the matter of the ambitions of Llywelyn of Wales?' John asked as he pressed home the point.

'Sire?' they asked in unison, mystified.

John gave them the look of a parent whose offspring have been caught out doing something they were expressly forbidden to do. 'I had an audience with FitzWalter yesterday, and he advises me that when you both called on him — *ahead* of reporting back here first, I note — you spoke of possible plans by the King of Wales to march on Pembroke, now that it's no longer defended by that traitor Marshal.'

'That is perhaps putting it too highly, sire,' Ranulf hastened to explain. 'It was merely the case that the steward of Pembroke mentioned to us that King Llywelyn has long admired the lush coastal estates of Pembroke, and would perhaps wish to join them with his Gwynedd lands, given that your daughter Joan is now queen of his mountainous lands to the north.'

'Regardless of his intentions, it is high time that I made a family visit to that part of the nation,' John replied coldly. 'Where better to approach Gwynedd than by way of Chester? Be prepared to meet me in Chester in two weeks' time, both of you. Ranulf shall be my host, and Hugh shall command my force. You are now dismissed.'

'At least we'll see our families again,' Hugh commented once they were outside.

Ranulf nodded, adding, 'Let's just hope that it's not for the last time.'

# XIII

Hugh and Ranulf dismounted and handed their mounts to the stable groom at the Flint Manor House. They turned as they heard a small voice call out, 'Is that my daddy?' A young girl scampered from the manor house doorway and raced towards them, hastily followed by Nan, hobbling as fast as her aged legs permitted. Behind her was Edwina, who rapidly overtook her just as their daughter Edith was being scooped up by Hugh in a loving embrace.

'And who are you, to be holding my daughter in your arms?' Edwina asked in a tone of mock severity that was neutralised by the broad smile that lit her face as Hugh walked towards her with Edith.

'I believe that I live here,' Hugh joked.

Edwina stepped back to look at him appraisingly as she continued the jest. 'My husband is away almost permanently, but you are handsome enough, so I'll have to make do with you in the meantime, assuming that you aren't planning on riding away again immediately after you've eaten.'

'We're on our way to Chester, certainly,' Hugh replied as he indicated Ranulf with a sideways nod, 'but I cannot resist the implied invitation to remain overnight, while my companion here journeys on. After we've *both* eaten, of course.'

'So what takes you to Chester, apart from enquiring as to whether or not we still have a son?' Edwina asked as they took it in turns to carve from the meat roast.

'The king is journeying into Wales, to issue a stern warning to King Llywelyn not to even *think* about marching south into Pembroke while its former earl and countess are away in

Ireland,' said Ranulf. 'Since my estates are a convenient stopping-off point on his westward travels, I must hasten home and advise my wife to kill the fatted calf and prepare the manor to receive a king.'

'You're *very* welcome to him as a house guest,' Edwina grimaced, 'but *must* Hugh go with you?'

'Into Wales, certainly, since he commands my force,' Ranulf reminded her, 'but at least he'll be reunited with Geoffrey, since we'll be taking men from the Chester garrison.'

'He has visited once or twice during your absence,' Edwina told Hugh, 'and he looks more like a true warrior each time. The boy has become a man, you'll find, and I only hope that you're not about to risk his life in some new military disaster of John's making.'

'I'll be by his side the whole time,' Hugh assured her.

She looked into his eyes with a reproving expression. 'So I'll be losing *both* of you in the same foolhardy enterprise, is that what you're telling me?'

'There should be no risk,' Ranulf intervened, 'other than catching an ague as we wander through windswept mountainous ranges where it rains every day, and twice on Sundays. The stated reason for the visit is in order for John to enquire as to the health of his daughter Joan, who's married to Llywelyn. He hasn't seen her since she left for her wedding some time ago.'

'He clearly has the same concern for his family as certain other people at Court that I could mention,' Edwina snorted as she punched Hugh playfully on the shoulder. 'But you can't have this one back for at least two days. One day to get over the shock of his return, and the second to remind him of what he'll be riding away from — *again*.'

Five days later Hugh and Ranulf were challenged at the huge double gates cut into the front wall of Chester Castle, at the top of the steep rise that was one of its greatest defensive assets. The young man challenging them was draped in the blue surcoat with three gold wheat sheafs that identified him as a man at arms of the Earldom of Chester. He was doing his best to appear formidable and challenging, but the suppressed humour was causing his lips to twitch involuntarily as Hugh fixed him with a stern gaze and asked, 'Since I never challenged you when you rode an imaginary broom horse around the hall in the Flint Manor House, why do you feel entitled to challenge me here as I seek to review my own men at arms?'

'Leave the boy be, Hugh,' Ranulf said. 'For one, he does not deserve it from the mouth of his own father; secondly, he is no boy anymore, and most importantly I am anxious for my dinner.'

Inside the Great Hall of Chester Castle, Constable Roger de Lacy smiled when Hugh enquired after Geoffrey's progress. 'I recall promising to return your son as a man, but in truth he was that when I first got him. His skill with arms speaks much for his early training at your hand, his courage is manifest, and his discipline is a great example to the others. For that reason, I have plans to promote him to Captain of the Guard when Ralph Treece takes his pension.'

'This is excellent news,' Hugh replied, 'and I thank you for offering him the opportunity that he has craved since he was seven years of age. Has he no flaws?'

De Lacy thought for a moment, then nodded. 'If you choose to call it a flaw, I believe that he lacks the brutality of your average man at arms. He is more likely to take a man prisoner than finish him off on the field of battle. Perhaps he gets that from you, or perhaps he should have taken holy orders or something.'

Hugh frowned. 'He is gifted with common humanity, that is all. If we do not encourage that in all our warriors, then battlefields become charnel houses, and entire communities are wiped out simply because they supplied hospitality to the enemy — sometimes unwillingly. I feel sure that you have personally witnessed the horror of wanton slaughter, rapine and butchery when soldiers are let loose on a captured town. With more men like Geoffrey in command, such obscenities may become a thing of the past.'

De Lacy replied, 'I need look no further for the source of your son's alleged flaw, although you seem to regard it as something laudable. However, you *did* ask.'

'And I respect your candour,' Hugh said. 'Now, how ready are the men to march west?'

'Whenever you command,' de Lacy replied, then coughed in embarrassment when he saw Ranulf's raised eyebrows. 'My apologies, my lord — it is of course for you to command them.'

'Ride at their head, you mean,' Ranulf replied. 'At least we are agreed on that, but they will in reality be commanded by Hugh, since I know as much about such things as I do about how to coax music from a citole. But if the men are ready, then I see no reason to delay, once the king has rested for a few days. He arrives on the morrow, and my larder will not sustain him and his entourage for longer than that.'

'You were right about the weather, at least,' Hugh grimaced as he lowered his head against the rain. 'Let us hope that our mounts can pick their way carefully over this goat track.'

They were somewhere on the rocky track that led to their destination, alongside the ocean from which the horizontal sheets of rain were driving into them from their right. Somewhere at the end of this road they hoped to reach the small town of Bangor, where King Llywelyn was said to be in residence at one of his several palaces.

In the lead were Ranulf and Hugh, their heads bowed against the elements, and immediately behind them rode Geoffrey, proudly at the head of the first two ranks of mounted men at arms from his Chester guard company. In the centre rode a dour-faced King John, the rain dripping from the rim of the fancy bonnet that now resembled a drowned cat. The two Court pages had long since abandoned any attempt to hold the protective canopy over John's head, after it had been blown out of their hands, several times, into the wild gorse and rocks to the left of the track. Behind him, the three ranks of the Earl of Chester's infantry kept their heads down, gaining no protection at all from the party ahead of them, given the sideways attack from the deluge.

Hugh raised his hand high in the air when, through the waterfall cascading from his helm, he spotted horsemen waiting ahead. Their leader challenged him in broken English, and Hugh managed to make out enough of what was being yelled at them over the noise of the rain to be able to respond that he was escorting the King of England, who was riding to Bangor to be reunited with his natural daughter, the Queen of Gwynedd. There was a favourable response; it seemed that their progress had been noted as far back as Abergele, and an escort had been sent out to guide them into Bangor.

Two hours later John had changed out of his soggy travel garments into suitable Court attire that was nevertheless damp, having travelled in the side pannier of a baggage horse. He was handed mugs of mulled and spiced wine that tasted like boiled nettles, but served to warm his innards, while his host Llywelyn enquired as to the reason for his visit.

'Is it not sufficient that I wished to lay eyes again on my only daughter?' John responded tersely.

Llywelyn was far from overawed, and replied with narrowed eyes, 'I thought you might have learned of my plans to encroach into Powys, now that Fadog has fallen to me.'

'I had not,' John replied haughtily, 'mainly because I have no interest in the petty squabbles of you mountain chieftains. What *does* interest me, however, is the suggestion that you might have ambitions to maraud further south, into my estates in Pembroke.'

'And why would I wish to do that?' Llywelyn asked with a stony face. 'I enjoy the warmest of relationships with Count William.'

'As I suspected,' John replied coldly. 'But since he is no longer infeft of Pembroke because I have taken it back on account of his treason, might that not cause you to renew your ambitions in that direction?'

'What ambition might that be?' Llywelyn asked guardedly. 'If, as you say, Pembroke is now yours once again, why would I incur the wrath of my wife's father, whose military strength is much greater than mine, by seeking to invade it?'

'Because it lies at the extremity of my Welsh lands,' John reminded him. 'And if, as you claim, you are close with William Marshal, why might you not seek to regain it for him?'

'Why has he displeased you?' Llywelyn countered.

John's face darkened in warning. 'That is no concern of yours if, as you claim, you have no interest in his fortunes. But I am proposing that we conclude a peace treaty while I am here, if only to reassure me that I need not look westwards for my enemies.'

'I would not rebel against my own father!' Joan protested, then fell instantly silent when ordered by John to do so.

He looked back questioningly at Llywelyn. 'Well?' he demanded.

Llywelyn nodded. 'If you wish. What terms do you propose?'

'A two-year truce. I will not ask that it be sworn on oath, since I am not even sure if Christianity has yet reached this benighted land of wind, rain and slate. Instead, I require hostages to your future good behaviour. Let us say thirty or so of the young sons of your leading chieftains.'

There was a sharp intake of breath from Joan, and Llywelyn's face paled, but he nevertheless nodded. 'You strike a hard bargain, but it shall be as you request. But give me a few days, and the boys may ride back in your train.'

Five days later they began the return journey, with several wagons having been added to their progress, containing twenty-eight Welsh youths, some as young as twelve, who gazed fearfully over the sides of their transports as the only land they had ever known fell away to the rear.

Geoffrey was swelling with pride as he guided his horse up and down the line of wagons containing the Welsh hostages. He had been personally selected by John to take command of the prisoner escort, and he was hoping that this would auger more responsibility within the royal army of which he hoped to become a senior commander like his father. He was allowed a brief one-day visit to his family home, then he was back in Chester Castle supervising the accommodation for their Welsh prisoners. They were not locked in dungeons, but it was doubtful that they regarded their bunks in the stable block, immediately above the horses, as appropriate for their rank as sons of mountain chieftains who served their king back in Gwynedd.

After only a few days of rest in Chester, and to Ranulf's profound relief, John announced his intention to travel east to his favourite castle at Nottingham. There he would meet with his Justiciar, Geoffrey FitzPeter, Earl of Essex, who had been commanded to ride north to meet the king and convey the latest tidings from London. Hugh rode back home with Geoffrey, who was brimming with the news that his commission had been extended, and he was ordered to continue on, first to Nottingham, and then down to London, in overall command of the Welsh boy hostages.

Edwina looked across the dinner table at him, concern in her eyes. 'Have you heard the expression that those who live by the sword are fated to die by the sword?' she asked him.

He shook his head. 'Who said that — the king?'

'It comes from holy scripture,' Hugh told him. 'And it comes close to the truth, so beware. I have been extremely fortunate not to have died several times while making my way in life as a soldier.'

'That was surely because of your skill with arms,' Geoffrey argued.

Hugh shrugged. 'There was also a good deal of luck involved, so always guard your back when on the field of battle. And, in another way, guard both your back *and* your tongue while in the royal presence. You may be in favour now, but that can change with one ill-considered word.'

'Your father speaks sense,' Edwina added. 'He did not get to attain his fifty-odd years without being both strong *and* cautious.'

'I was also never brutal,' Hugh added as he recalled what he had learned in Chester. 'I was advised by Roger de Lacy that you lack the brutality that often comes with being a fearless warrior. Do not regard that as a failing, if you wish to retain your self-respect and preserve your soul from sinking into the pit of Hell.'

'Such poetry, and from a man at arms!' Geoffrey replied admiringly. 'But I thank you for that welcome advice, since I have often worried regarding my distaste for cruelty that is not warranted. Once you have beaten your man fairly in battle, there is no need to butcher him.'

Edwina gave a faint cry, and her hand flew to her mouth.

Geoffrey looked embarrassed and ashamed and rose from the table to comfort her. 'Apologies, Mother. We should perhaps have had our conversation in private.'

'Just see that you heed your father's sage advice,' she mumbled through rising tears as she raced from the hall, leaving father and son staring at each other.

It was Hugh who broke the awkward silence. 'See to it that you never lose that feeling of mercy for those whose lives you hold in your hands,' he told him. 'And be sure to give your mother a big hug and comforting words ere you depart on the morrow.'

# XIV

A week passed, during which Hugh revelled in the luxury of having no duties to perform. Ranulf's men had been placed under the temporary command of a very proud Geoffrey of Flint as they made the cross-country journey to Nottingham with their prisoners. Then ten days after Geoffrey had bidden them farewell, Hugh came sleepily down the stairs at daybreak to find the steward standing awkwardly to attention by the fireplace in which the kindling had just been lit. Their eyes met, and Hugh could detect bad tidings in those of the steward.

'What is it?' he demanded hoarsely.

'Young Master Geoffrey, Master. In the stables.'

'Is he hurt?'

'Not that I could see, Master. But he was sobbing fit to burst.'

Hugh raced out in his hose, not even bothering to climb into his boots by the front door. He found Geoffrey seated on a hay bale, doubled over as if in pain, and he ran over to him. Geoffrey raised his head to look up at him, his pale face raw at the eyes and nostrils.

'What ails you?' Hugh demanded. 'You look like a man on the edge of death.'

'I am probably marked for death,' Geoffrey replied hollowly. 'I can no longer serve a butcher. I've deserted the king's service, and sooner or later they will come for me here.'

Hugh took a seat next to Geoffrey as he tried to absorb the full import of the terrible confession.

Geoffrey finally broke the chilling silence. 'Do you not wish to know why?'

'I feel sure that you will tell me eventually,' Hugh replied, 'but my first concern is to see to your safe hiding. It cannot be here, clearly, and your mother must not know.'

'This was the only place I could think of,' Geoffrey explained. 'I hope I will not bring disgrace upon the family.'

Hugh gave a hollow laugh. 'Disgrace is the least of my concerns — I am more anxious to ensure that you remain alive. What you have done may be forgiven in time, but the king's first reaction is likely to be a blind rage in which he could not be persuaded towards any act of mercy.'

'It was just such an act that led to my desertion,' Geoffrey replied miserably. 'I could no longer serve such a fiend.'

Both men started as they sensed movement at the stable door, then heaved sighs of relief when they realised that it was only the stable groom, Tom, who was returning to his loft above the horses clutching a chunk of bread and a mug of ale, his customary breakfast. He hesitated when he became aware of Hugh and Geoffrey seated on hay bales, and Hugh called him over.

'Is Cook already at work?' he asked.

Tom nodded. 'She's just baking fresh bread, and Polly's already milked the cows, Master.'

'This is good,' Hugh said. 'Now, I want you to go back to the kitchen and ask Cook for bread, cheese and ale. Do not reveal that you have seen Master Geoffrey, understood? Make out that the victuals are for me alone, and that I'm hungry. There's a whole shilling in it for you if you succeed. Now off you go.'

Tom scampered off, and Hugh turned back to Geoffrey.

'You clearly cannot remain here, and I have just thought of something. But first I need to know the reason for your desertion, although I suspect that it was a just one.'

Geoffrey nodded, and his face grew paler as he recounted the events that had led to such a serious action on his part. 'When we reached Nottingham, the Justiciar was waiting with ill tidings. It seems that two of the nation's leading barons had been detected plotting against the king's life, and seeking to persuade the Mayor of London to enlist the merchants in some sort of uprising. That was bad enough, but John flew into an even greater rage when he learned that the two men responsible — FitzWalter and de Vesci — had escaped, and were rumoured to be heading for Wales. That was when John became totally uncontrollable, and gave orders that the boy hostages were to be hung from the castle walls. It was horrible!'

Tears began rolling down his cheeks, and his body shook as he recalled what followed.

'Their screams and pleas for mercy were terrible to hear. Just mere boys, away from their families, most not even with their first beards. I refused to obey the order, and was dismissed from my post. I would have been taken up myself had it not been for John's need to order the castle guard to do his filthy deed. They secured ropes to the curtain wall, threw a noose around the neck of each lad, then heaved them over. Dear God in Heaven forgive me, but I just ran — grabbed my horse from the stable and pounded up the road through the Shire Wood until I reached the track that led to Buxton, and hence north from there. I have been riding for almost three days, and my horse is spent.'

Tom reappeared with a basket full of bread, cheese and ale. Geoffrey grabbed the food gratefully and began to stuff it into his mouth, until cautioned by his father that he would give himself stomach pains if he continued in that vein. 'I need you in good fettle to return from where you came, more or less,' he added.

Geoffrey cleared his mouth of cheese as he opened it to protest. 'If I return to Nottingham I shall be taken up, and probably roasted. It is rumoured to be one of the king's favourite punishments for desertion.'

'His cruelty and wickedness will one day be his downfall,' Hugh predicted gloomily. 'But I was not suggesting that you return to the town. It is time for a visit to your Uncle Robert.'

'Repton?' Geoffrey queried. 'Would John not think to look for me there?'

'What makes you think that capturing you will be at the forefront of his plans?' Hugh replied with raised eyebrows and a knowing smile. 'He has a rebellion to put down, as you yourself advise me. I heard while in Chester that he has been excommunicated by the Pope, and the nation placed under interdict, because of his refusal to accept Langton as Archbishop of Canterbury. Compared with matters of such gravity, the desertion of one man at arms will seem as nothing. A mere fly to be swatted away when he has the time. But you will not be staying on the manor grounds at Repton.'

'Where, then?' Geoffrey asked, at a loss to understand what his father had in mind.

Hugh smiled reassuringly. 'Not long after you were born, during the reign of King Richard, John maintained a stronghold at Nottingham Castle, under the protection of the man who was then its sheriff and constable. That same sheriff — a man named de Wendenal — persecuted the landholders for miles around, and particularly those in the Shire Wood that you recently rode through. But they fought back by forming their own army of "outlaws", as they were called, and they were crucial to the storming and recovery of the castle when

King Richard returned. I was part of the force that lay siege to the castle, and the so-called outlaws were pardoned by King Richard, and given back their lands. However, I have no doubt that their burning hatred for John, and their bitter memories of his cruelty towards them, have not diminished over the years, and that one or more of them would be happy to hide a fugitive from his justice, if you could call it that.'

'So I am to live like a vagabond outlaw, haunting the hedgerows and robbing travellers?' Geoffrey asked fearfully.

Hugh shook his head. 'Far from it. I believe that you will be welcomed with open arms onto one or other of their restored estates, as the son and grandson of the men who secured their freedom — an action that led indirectly to your grandfather's death, thereby leaving a debt to be repaid by them. You have been raised on an estate, and can earn your keep tending cattle, sheep, goats and horses, or felling trees.'

'Forever?' Geoffrey asked gloomily.

'No, until such time as the air has cleared, John has come to his senses, the nation is once more at rest, and honest men can go about their rightful business.'

'I doubt that such a day is on the immediate horizon. What do you intend to do in the meantime?'

'What I was bidden to do,' Hugh replied. 'It was John's intention to take his prisoners south, and journey to London by way of Norwich, where Uncle Ranulf and I were ordered to join him after we had rested following our journey into Wales. I shall journey to Norwich as planned, pretend no knowledge of your desertion, and do what I can to preserve John from himself, for the sake of the nation.'

Hugh opted to say nothing even to Ranulf about Geoffrey's desertion, but merely recounted what he had heard of the state of the realm from those travelling to Repton from Nottingham. When Ranulf queried why Hugh had been in Repton, he explained it away as a routine family visit.

'I have a brother who I see all too infrequently, as you know,' he reasoned, 'and in these uncertain times, who knows when, or if, we shall see each other again?'

'You believe things to be so bad?' Ranulf asked as they saw the spires of Norwich emerge from the morning mist a few miles to the south of them.

'We know of at least a dozen of the nation's leading barons who are on the point of rebellion. Two of them have already tried unsuccessfully, and even if their lands be forfeit, as they almost certainly will be, that will not prevent them playing upon their family connections. Most of them were related by marriage, if you recall?'

Ranulf nodded. 'There is also the effect of the interdict. On my own Cheshire estate there have been strident complaints brought to me, and requests that I intervene with John to have the interdict lifted. While it obtains, there can be no lawful marriages, no baptisms and no burials according to Christian rites. Since bodies cannot be allowed to mount up in rotting piles, there have been many informal burials. Honest men fear for the souls of their loved ones who now lie under unmarked mounds of earth, unshriven and without Masses. That is as great a source of unrest throughout the realm as unjust taxation.'

Hugh sighed. 'Would that we could talk some sense into John. Even *common* sense would suffice.'

'We would first need to teach him humility,' Ranulf chuckled despite the seriousness of the situation. 'Would *you* wish to volunteer for that task?'

Once they reached Norwich and reported for duty, word was sent to their temporary chambers that John wished to see them without delay. They each had good reason to be apprehensive of what the audience might bring, and Hugh was bracing himself to lie convincingly about Geoffrey's desertion. When they approached the dais on which John was seated, bowed the knee, kissed the hand and kept their eyes on the floor, they were all but trembling, and ill-prepared for the king's first question.

'How soon could you prepare for a foray into Poitou, and how many men could you bring to my battle banner?'

'Sire?' Ranulf eventually asked as he looked disbelievingly up at the throne.

John glared down at him. 'Have I lost the power of speech, or have you recently incurred a loss of hearing?'

'You wish to mount a campaign into Poitou?' Hugh asked.

John frowned. '*You* at least heard what I said. You have not lost your hearing, but you are currently missing a son, are you not?'

'Sire?' was all that Hugh could offer by way of reply, as Ranulf turned his downcast head to look at him enquiringly.

'Your traitor of a son, who deserted my service at Nottingham, despite the trust I placed in him, and the honour I bestowed upon him by putting him in charge of the Welsh boys.'

'I was unaware of any desertion, sire,' Hugh lied.

John brought his fist down hard on the arm of his throne. 'Whether I choose to believe you or not, you should know that his life is forfeit if ever he is caught. No doubt he is conspiring with the rebels even as we speak.'

'Rebels, sire?' Ranulf asked innocently.

This time, John leapt from his seat as he shrieked, 'Yes — rebels! Where have you been for the past month — in a nunnery?'

'We are only just returned from our estates, sire,' Hugh reminded him, but this did not serve to abate the royal ire as John continued to thunder down at them.

'Robert FitzWalter and Eustace de Vesci! They conspired during my absence from Westminster, and were it not for Justiciar FitzPeter's close relationship with the Mayor of London I would not have known of their plot against my life. My *life*, mark you! I will have them put to death in the most painful and humiliating manner that can be devised once they are caught, but God alone knows how far the poison may have spread! What I propose is to summon every available noble in the realm to my standard and march back into France, there to demonstrate to the Christian world that King John of England is not a man to trifle with. Those who cannot — or will not — supply the men shall provide the coin for mercenaries from the Low Countries.'

'Another scutage tax?' Ranulf asked timorously as the colour drained from his face.

John nodded. 'In your case it will of course be men at arms and weaponry, and your force shall be led by the Earl of Flint here, unless he is too busy hiding his chicken-livered son from my wrath. On your feet, both of you, and see to the task I have set you. The troops will be assembled at Winchester one month from now.'

As they wandered down the outside corridor like two men in the grip of a nightmare, Ranulf turned to Hugh.

'Why did Geoffrey desert? And do not feign ignorance with me, Hugh — we've been close friends for too long.'

Hugh hesitated briefly, then drew Ranulf into an alcove as he asked, 'Have you heard ought of the Welsh hostages since we arrived here?'

'We've been here less than a day, Hugh, so why would I have done?'

'Well, they are dead. Hung from the walls of Nottingham Castle, on John's order. An order he gave to Geoffrey, who had not the stomach for it.'

'Dear God!' Ranulf muttered. 'I knew that his reluctance to engage in acts of butchery would be the end of him, but so soon?'

'Fear not for him, Ranulf, for he is safely hidden, although I dare not reveal his whereabouts, even to you. Let us worry instead how to prevent this latest madness. We could not sustain an army against Philip of France for a week, as you well know. How do we talk him out of it?'

'I would rather place my hand in the mouth of a rabid dog than attempt that. Perhaps we should pray.'

'You forget that the churches are closed,' Hugh said grimly. 'Any miracles will need to be wrought by men rather than by God. Anyway, let us go in search of dinner, assuming that we can also find our appetites.'

Two days later, the miracle that they had been awaiting came from an unlikely source. They were taking supper together in Ranulf's chamber when Justiciar FitzPeter was admitted, and accepted their invitation to join them at board. As he carved away calmly at a side of pork, FitzPeter quietly asked, 'Could you put together an escort to Dover, should I request one in the king's name?'

'If His Majesty approves of it, most certainly,' Ranulf agreed as he mentally tallied how many men at arms he had brought with him down to Norwich.

'It will be to escort the king himself,' FitzPeter replied quietly. 'No-one is to know of it.'

'Why the secrecy?' Hugh asked.

FitzPeter frowned. 'It's to save John's face.'

'What is being planned?' Ranulf pressed. 'A swift invasion force across the Channel?'

'No, a meeting with a Papal Legate in the Templar Church. I believe I have all but succeeded in persuading John to accept Stephen Langton as our new Archbishop of Canterbury.'

'Pray to God that you have,' Ranulf muttered, 'if it will mean the lifting of the interdict.'

'It will mean much more than that,' FitzPeter told them. 'It will almost certainly lift the excommunication order on John, which will mean that the remaining monarchs of Christendom will not be honour bound to unseat him. It may even mean that His Holiness can be persuaded to issue a Bull banning any rebellion, on pain of further excommunication. And we might even look forward to Langton bringing his serene counsels to bear upon John himself, who seems destined to provoke a nationwide rebellion with his ill-tempered policies.'

It was all achieved within the month, and the new Archbishop of Canterbury, Stephen Langton, lost no time in attempting to modify John's extreme attitude towards those who seemed unprepared to support his ambition to win back the lands he had lost. It was Langton who restrained John's impulse to strike, first at Llywelyn of Wales, then at the northern barons who were the most vociferous in their refusal to supply either men at arms or finance for the venture back across the Channel.

As if determined to demonstrate his ability to prevail over Philip of France without any support from within England, John sent numerous envoys into the Low Countries and beyond in order to establish an alliance of rulers who had reasons of their own to wish to see Philip's power curtailed, since it threatened to burst out of the Île-de-France into new territories.

Leaving Ranulf and Hugh behind in England to organise against any uprising during his absence, John joined Holy Roman Emperor Otto IV of Germany, the Counts of Flanders, Boulogne and Holland, and the Dukes of Lorraine and Limburg in a combined force that began to slowly lumber out of Flanders with its sights set on Paris. It had only reached Bouvines, on the borders of Belgium and France, when the faster, more experienced and better led mounted forces of Philip of France smashed into the largely infantry ranks of the hastily assembled allied forces. They inflicted such a humiliating defeat upon them that John was obliged to agree to peace terms that included the surrender of Anjou, the last remaining English possession across the Channel, and the spiritual birthplace of the once mighty Angevin Empire begun by John's great-grandfather.

His humiliation complete, John returned to England determined to wreak vengeance on those who had failed to rally to his cause, and were now sniggering at his downfall across the water.

# XV

While there had never been a good time to be in King John's service, this moment was arguably the worst. With heavy hearts and fear for their own lives, Hugh and Ranulf obeyed the call to a meeting of a hastily constructed and urgently summoned King's Council at Oxford.

Hugh looked askance down the long table that contained many unfamiliar faces, and a few that he knew to be those of high-ranking nobles. They were seated in the Great Hall of Oxford Castle, and King John was at the head of the table, grim-faced and pale. Ranulf was seated next to Hugh, who leaned slightly towards him and asked softly, 'Who are all these people, and why am I here?'

Ranulf replied, 'You are here because you lead my force, which is the largest of any privately raised army in the nation, and I am here because I am one of the most prominent barons who remains loyal to John. As for the rest, the remarkably young-looking cleric sitting opposite is Walter de Gray, Bishop of Worcester and nephew of the Bishop of Norwich, who almost became our Archbishop of Canterbury. Walter is currently Chancellor of England, and the new Archbishop of Canterbury, Stephen Langton, you already know.'

'Who are the two who are arguing as if they dislike each other intensely?' Hugh asked as he nodded towards the two red-faced nobles further down on the opposite side.

'Well deduced. They hate the sight of each other, but have been ordered to this meeting on pain of banishment back to their lands in Poitou and Touraine. The older of the two is Peter des Roches, the newly appointed Justiciar following

FitzPeter's death. The other man is Hubert de Burgh, Custodian of the Welsh Marches, who firmly believes that he should have been appointed as Justiciar.'

'And the king hopes to face his current crisis with such a dissolute assembly?'

'He has little choice, remember,' Ranulf reminded him. 'As the old adage goes, "Needs must when the Devil is on your tail".'

'Must I wait until this convention of fishwives has finished exchanging the latest gossip?' John bellowed down the table. It fell instantly silent as he glared at each of them in turn. 'You are what remains of those who have chosen to honour their pledge at my coronation. You are here to support me against those who fondly believe that they may continue to live under my protection while contributing nothing towards it. Do we know which slimy rock they are currently hiding under?'

A polite cough from Ranulf caused all eyes to turn to him. 'My scouts advise me that there is a large assembly of them gathered in Northampton,' he announced.

'The best estimate is a thousand armed men, under various liveries,' Hugh added.

'Do they have a leader?' John asked.

Ranulf swallowed hard before replying, 'Two, sire. Robert FitzWalter and Eustace de Vesci.'

John let out a stream of foul invective that brought blushes to the faces of the clergymen gathered around the table, then finally declaimed, 'I should have hung that cowardly bastard FitzWalter after he surrendered Vaudreuil to France. As for de Vesci, he's too close with the Scots king after marrying his whore of a half-sister. Who else?'

It fell silent, as those in the know became reluctant to name names with which they might be too closely associated themselves. Eventually, as John's face grew redder and redder, Ranulf offered a few more possibilities, after first coughing nervously.

'As you will be aware, sire, the Earl of Flint and myself toured the nation on your behalf, in order to sound out the likely response to further taxation ahead of your plans to invade Normandy…'

'Yes, yes — just get *on* with it, man!' John yelled. 'Either name names this instant or I will have your tongue cut out!'

Hugh decided to come to Ranulf's rescue. 'Almost certainly Saer de Quincy, sire, since he was the one, along with FitzWalter, who surrendered Vaudreuil, and he has a grievance regarding the withholding of one of his Leicester estates. Then there's Geoffrey de Mandeville, who was related by marriage for some years to FitzWalter, and is now married to your former queen and deeply in your debt. I also suspect Henry de Bohun, Earl of Hereford, Richard de Clare of Tonbridge, William d'Albini, who's FitzWalter's cousin, along with D'Albini's nephew Robert de Ros and his close friend William de Mowbray…'

'Enough!' John bellowed as he brought his fist down so hard on the table that wine spilled from his goblet. 'If they are in Northampton, barely a day's hard ride from here, and they have only a thousand under arms, why may we not smoke them out?'

It fell so silent that it was possible to hear the nervous breathing of those assembled, and all eyes turned to Hugh, who shrugged.

'It is one of the most difficult castles in the realm to approach with a large force,' he explained. 'There are deep trenches that become moats when the nearby river, with which they are connected, overflows. Our strength lies in cavalry; this would be useless in any attack on Northampton, which would need to be by siege. Unfortunately the town itself is to the rear of the castle, which makes it all too easy for those within to obtain supplies.'

'Not if we sack the town, and burn it to the ground,' John retorted, only to have the restraining hand of Stephen Langton placed on the sleeve of his robe.

'I fear that His Holiness would disapprove of such wanton cruelty to innocent souls,' the archbishop murmured.

John shook his hand free as he hissed back, 'They are hardly "innocent" if they support treasonous dogs. If they harbour traitors, then they may die like traitors.'

Hugh glanced at Ranulf with an expression of helplessness, but his companion had been thinking it through and offered an alternative.

'Why do we not lure them out of there by exposing ourselves to attack?' he suggested. 'Then Hugh and his forces may turn on them and wipe them away.'

'You seriously suggest that I make myself a target for these ingrates?' John demanded.

Hugh leapt to his defence. 'It is a well-practised tactic of warfare, sire.'

'And how do we know that we are at war with them, anyway?' John thundered. 'Has anyone enquired of them why they are rebelling in this outrageous fashion?'

'I think we know why, Your Majesty,' Langton murmured. 'They have had enough of being taxed, and they cannot see any advantage to be gained from it, given the unfortunate outcome of your recent foray across the Channel.'

John glared at Langton, but didn't reply, and Ranulf picked up the point.

'I could send someone to parley with them, sire,' he suggested. 'Then we might find some way through this impasse.'

'I already suggested one,' John retorted. 'Burn them out!'

'His Holiness would react badly, sire,' Langton reminded him.

John's fist came down heavily on the table once more as he bellowed, 'You can all rot in Hell!'

He leaped up angrily and stormed out through the back door that led to his private chambers before anyone could even rise to give the customary bow. In the stunned silence that descended on the assembly, the only one to speak was Archbishop Langton, who smiled wanly at Ranulf as he made a suggestion.

'Might we leave you to parley with the rebels as you offered, my Lord Ranulf?'

'Even if I do, will His Majesty listen to their demands?' Ranulf asked with a defeated look.

'Leave John to me. He may not respect the Pope's holiness, but he fears his influence. Perhaps that might be employed for a positive purpose for once.'

The rebel barons had been meeting daily for many hours at a time. Their final list of demands was almost complete when Robert FitzWalter was advised by the castellan that two envoys had arrived from the king. He agreed to meet with them, and as Ranulf and Hugh were admitted to the Great Hall, he grinned.

'I wish I had risked a wager on you two being sent by Lackland. What has he promised you for risking your lives? Whatever it be, let me assure you from bitter experience that he will renege on the promise and find some spurious grounds on which to have you disgraced and indebted to him. Some wine before you grovel?'

'We do not come to grovel,' Ranulf replied sternly. 'Whatever may be your opinion of our king and those who serve him, honour requires that you allow us to depart unharmed once we have completed our business.'

'I'm mightily surprised that anyone employed in conducting John's business still retains any concept of honour, but be that as it may, what are his terms for surrender?'

'I was not aware that your grievances had grown into a war,' Hugh responded. 'As you will have observed, there are fewer than a handful of armed men in my party, and we come in the spirit of compromise. What we military men call a "parley".'

'Put another way,' Ranulf added, 'what is your list of grievances?'

'How many days have you put aside to learn of them?' FitzWalter sneered. 'We have composed a list that is so long that were we to hang it from the ceiling, it would gather dust as it trailed across the floor.'

'You have a copy of that list that we may take back to the king?' Ranulf asked.

FitzWalter turned to a page who had been standing silently in one corner of the chamber and instructed him to seek out Richard de Clare. 'Obtain from him the fair copy of our Great Charter.'

Hugh and Ranulf returned to Oxford, and only then did they open the scroll that they'd been handed. They read it in mounting disbelief, then requested an urgent meeting with Archbishop Langton, who listened calmly to their concerns and offered to accompany them when they presented it to the king. Langton was the only one exhibiting a calm face as they tremblingly handed over the list of the barons' demands, hoping that John would bear in mind that they were only the messengers.

As John quickly ran his eyes down the parchment, his face grew darker and darker. Finally he hurled the list to the floor and glared at the three anxious men who had brought it into the Audience Chamber.

'They might as well just cut off my balls right now!' he yelled. 'If I agree to this list of outrageous demands, I will no longer be King of England! Well? Did they seriously believe that I would agree to it?'

'Sire,' Langton replied calmly, 'if you take a moment to consider the essence of what they are politely requesting, as loyal subjects, it is no more than you swore to give them as part of your coronation vows, taken before God.'

'I thought that God would be dragged into it ere long,' John snarled, 'but I had not expected it to be so soon. Pray tell me how these impudent attempts to geld me can possibly be justified by reference to the promises I gave at my coronation.'

'Let us consider each of them in turn,' Langton suggested without any indication that he felt intimidated by the royal anger. 'The most fundamental is a demand — no, let us call it a reminder that when you were crowned king, you swore a holy oath to uphold the laws and customs of the realm. There was also an undertaking to deal with each man, rich or poor, according to the law that governed his transgressions, and not by any arbitrary will. You also promised equal access to the king's justice to all men, regardless of their circumstances, coupled with a promise that no-one might be punished without being adjudged guilty of some offence recognised by the law of the realm.'

'There was something there also preventing me from raising taxes in order to defend my lands, was there not?' John demanded suspiciously.

Langton nodded. 'Indeed there was, sire. But it merely requires that the barons be consulted before any future tax is imposed.'

'And why should I stoop to do that?' John demanded. 'They would be bound to reject it. Is that why they drivel on about some sort of Council of Barons?'

'That is simply in order that there may be a process whereby new taxes can be approved,' Langton attempted to reassure him. 'You would be in favour of the approval of new taxes, surely?'

John glared at him. 'You miss the point, Archbishop. When I need to impose a new tax, it is because I deem it to be in my best interests, which means the best interests of the nation. Why should I seek the approval of a knot of ill-disposed whiners who simply wish to preserve their own wealth, contrary to the best interests of England?'

'It would be for you to persuade them to your cause, sire,' was all that Langton could offer.

John turned his gaze on Ranulf and Hugh. 'What say you? Do you wish to see your king reduced to the status of a peasant with a begging bowl?'

'Speaking for myself, and hopefully, in your eyes, as a leading baron of the realm,' Ranulf replied tactfully, 'I have never doubted that the raising of an army requires wealth. As one who is already blessed with such a force, of course, I have never been called upon to pay scutage, but were I called upon to do so, then my loyalty to Your Majesty…'

'What say you?' John cut him off with a raised hand as he turned to Hugh, who shrugged.

'As a man of warfare, I simply ask this: what is our position if you decline to accede to the barons' demands? Do we yet know their strength of arms? Their numbers? Their current location?'

'I may be of assistance in that,' Langton interjected. 'I am fortunate that my network of bishoprics and holy houses enables messengers to pass back and forth between me and other parts of the realm. So far, or so I have been advised, most of the Eastern counties have pledged allegiance to the rebels, who in the main come from the north of the nation. They are strong in both Lincoln and Norwich, and — as we know — they are secure behind the walls of Northampton, from which they can send messengers into the Midlands. Then there is London…'

'What of London?' John demanded.

Langton bowed his head. 'Its bishop advises me that the merchants have given a pledge to open the city gates should it be demanded of them by the rebels, sire. They are much distressed by the prospect of more taxation, or perhaps a further disruption of trade should a civil war break out, and they seek to have the uncertainty resolved as soon as possible. They have been assured by FitzWalter that there will be no new taxes, and that trade with the Low Countries can be guaranteed for the future once a commitment is given to Philip of France that we have no remaining interest in retaking your father's former possessions.'

'Bastards!' John yelled as he hurled his wine mug at the side tapestries. 'Traitors, every one of them! They have sold me out for a few bales of wool! They will pay dearly for this!'

'Be that as it may, sire,' Hugh offered as he crossed his fingers behind his back, 'there remains the issue of where we should best locate ourselves to meet any armed uprising.'

'They wouldn't dare!' John insisted, then looked enquiringly back at Hugh as he added, 'Would they?'

'I cannot give any guarantee on that score, sire,' Hugh replied as he racked his brains for something more reassuring. 'I can only speak as an experienced man at arms. It is my humble and most loyal opinion that we should remove ourselves further from Oxford, which as you reminded us only recently is barely a day's ride from Northampton.'

'Wallingford!' John suggested as his eyes glinted. 'It has ever been a royal castle, and has never once been successfully besieged!'

Hugh shook his head gently as his military sense clicked in. 'Sire, you would be exposed to attack from the west, and it would be easy for the enemy to march across from Northampton while you have only the river ford at your back. And given the lack of recent rain, the ford would be easy to cross from the London side.'

'At least you concede that the barons are now our enemies,' John replied curtly, annoyed that he was yet again being corrected in his military judgment. 'Where, then?'

'Perhaps Windsor, sire,' Hugh replied, more confident of his ground. 'It can be heavily garrisoned, and it has the broader reach of the Thames in front of it, which will impede any approach from either Northampton or the city. It is well stocked against any siege, and it has a well-trained and well-disciplined royal guard.'

'Langton?' John asked.

The archbishop nodded. 'I can see no reason against such a suggestion, made by an experienced soldier, sire.'

Several weeks later, after much diplomatic movement to and fro, the rebel barons assembled at the village of Staines, to the south-east of Windsor, under the unchallenged leadership of Robert FitzWalter, who was now calling himself Marshal of the Army of God. They had been issued with bonds of safe conduct drawn up by Ranulf, who by this seemingly generous ruse acquired the names of all those who had thrown in their lot with FitzWalter. He was concerned to note among them the name of John de Lacy, the son of the man who had been Constable of Chester Castle until his recent death. Ranulf was de Lacy's feudal overlord and had accepted his oath of fealty, only to learn that the king had demanded seven thousand marks in return for admitting him to an inheritance that the law regarded as automatically his. Little wonder that so many barons were on the point of armed rebellion, Ranulf reflected sadly, when the law was being manipulated and abused in such a fashion. Little wonder that their demands were basically only a plea for justice under the coronation oath that John had sworn.

Once the barons were assembled, and had pitched their tents in and around the village that sat on the banks of the Thames a few miles downstream from Windsor, word was sent to John that they were ready to meet with him. He in turn ordered that a small marquee be erected in the flat meadow known as Runnymede, which lay on the far bank of the river close to the village of Egham. Once it was prepared, and after last-minute adjustments, by clerks on both sides, to the actual wording of what was now being referred to as 'The Great Charter', John rode out from Windsor with a large company of men at arms, accompanied by Langton, Ranulf and Hugh. He sat inside the marquee on the throne had that had been transported by wagon as part of the sedate, and seemingly reluctant, progress from the castle.

FitzWalter was granted admission to the royal presence, along with Geoffrey de Mandeville and Saer de Quincy. John looked up with a snarling countenance as they entered, and muttered, 'The dogs have finally come to the heel of the master, who throws them this bone. Mind that it does not choke your poxy throats.' He then affixed the royal seal onto the foot of the signed Charter, then nudged it forward on the table that had been brought for the occasion.

The barons' delegation left with the sealed Charter in their hands, smirks on their faces, and not even the suggestion of a bow. John sat back in his chair with a sigh, as Langton was the first to congratulate him on his wisdom and courtly humility. 'England is all the greater for this, sire,' he oozed as he bowed from the presence back into the afternoon sun, leaving just Ranulf and Hugh.

'May I echo the words of the archbishop?' Ranulf murmured.

John snorted. 'You may if you wish, but I did not think you were so easily duped.'

'Sire?' Ranulf asked.

John laughed unpleasantly. 'I have simply signed and sealed the Charter, you fool. That doesn't mean that I intend to abide by it.'

# XVI

In the weeks that followed, those within the inner circle at Court waited for some indication that what had been agreed at Runnymede would be implemented. In particular, both Hugh and Ranulf found it difficult to believe that John had actually agreed to a charter that established a Barons' Council that was to be summoned to advise the king and give approval before important measures were introduced, such as the raising of new taxes. Their scepticism was justified late one afternoon when they were summoned to Lambeth Palace, the recently acquired London residence of the Archbishop of Canterbury on the south bank of the Thames.

'I fear that John has fooled us all,' Archbishop Langton announced with a gloom-laden countenance after they had each kissed his pontifical ring of office and taken a seat.

'We suspected as much, after he failed to summon the Barons' Council before imposing another scutage tax to pay for more mercenaries from Poitou,' Ranulf replied, 'but how does he justify such an early breach of the Great Charter?'

'He went behind my back, direct to Rome,' Langton admitted with a long face. 'Unknown — and, I have to say unbidden — by me, he pledged England to the Pope, in effect swearing fealty to him, and offering to go on Crusade. Pope Innocent was all too easily seduced into believing that he had brought an infamous agnostic into the fold. Now John has appealed to him for relief from the consequences of the Charter, and His Holiness has not only absolved John from all its clauses, but has excommunicated those barons who forced him to sign it. We must, I fear, prepare for renewed armed conflict, which is why I have summoned you here, in order that you may make the necessary arrangements.'

Hugh and Ranulf exchanged uneasy glances, before Ranulf disclosed more bad news.

'It may already have begun, Your Grace. I received word this morning that Llywelyn of Wales has finally reacted to the disgraceful hanging of the hostages and is amassing his forces. I can only assume that the first target will be Chester, where unfortunately there is currently no constable in command of the castle. Roger de Lacy died some time ago, and his son John is one of the rebel barons. I was about to head north with Hugh at the head of my men at arms, in order to prepare the castle for a siege.'

'You will be too late to retake Rochester, then,' Langton nodded sadly, and when both men raised their eyebrows, he went on, 'I had left it unguarded, and my constable, unknown to me, had sided with the rebels who still hold London while John skulks in Windsor. He opened the gates to them, and they now have a firm stronghold between the king and any possible further recruits from Poitou.'

'Is John aware of this?' Ranulf asked.

Langton shook his head. 'That is why I summoned you both here, and God be praised that you opted to take the route through Surrey, since all of London north of the river is in rebel hands. But I require you to advise John of the loss of Rochester, and persuade him to retake it, if we are to have an open road to the Channel ports in Kent.'

'Will you also advise him of the threat from Wales?' Hugh asked Ranulf as they rode back through Chertsey.

Ranulf shook his head. 'John is not the best man to whom to impart more than one item of bad tidings at the same time, as you are aware. Langton has a very good point regarding the value of Rochester castle as a fortress guarding the Dover Road. We must persuade John to retake it as soon as possible.'

In the event, John needed little persuasion, and in one of his more successful military exploits he was back inside its walls within weeks of his arrival, accompanied by Ranulf's force, heavily supplemented by Poitevin mercenaries. In reality the military genius was Hugh's. He quickly came to appreciate that the rebels to whom they were about to lay siege could only receive reinforcements, and fresh supplies, from their main body now holding London. This would necessitate them crossing the Medway by the old wooden bridge that gave access to the castle, and once his forces had crossed, he ordered that the bridge be burned down behind them.

They then faced the formidable task of storming a castle that had been built to withstand a siege, with the main entrance on the first floor, battlements from which bowmen could spray deadly shafts down on any invaders, and walls twelve feet thick. Hugh adapted a technique he had heard was employed in the Holy Land, and he persuaded John to recruit men with hammers and axes from the nearby township, who dug under the walls until their wooden support beams were exposed. They were then smeared with pig fat and set alight. When the south-east tower collapsed, the rebels inside were forced into the remaining section of the keep, from which supplies were withheld until impending starvation and 'siege fever' forced an inglorious surrender. Rochester was back in royal hands, and Hugh was the hero of the hour.

Realising, very belatedly, that he had men about him who knew more about warfare than he did, John accepted Hugh's advice that they now divide their forces. A detachment was sent under the command of John's half-brother William Longespée to bottle up the rebels in North London then proceed to East Anglia in order to mop up the few known rebels who had not joined the main force. Meanwhile, Ranulf and Hugh headed the bulk of John's army on a long journey north, to the hotbeds of revolt in Yorkshire, Lancashire and the North Midlands.

Everywhere they journeyed, the story was the same: the 'Lord' had joined the rebels and had taken himself down to London. Unable to arrest anyone for treason on the estates they visited, John grew more and more frustrated. Ranulf and Hugh urged him not to take it out on those who remained on the estates that he declared forfeit, and they ordered the stewards to remit the estate revenues to the Exchequer.

Once they reached Nottingham, the king was easily prevailed upon to take some time to indulge in hunting at his favourite lodge in the Shire Wood, not without some apprehension on Hugh's part that Geoffrey might be discovered there. But the brief royal sojourn gave the two cousins time to visit their homes in Chester and Flint. For Hugh it was a bittersweet homecoming, given the need to keep from Edwina the fact that their son had deserted the royal service and was in hiding. He succeeded in persuading his wife that Geoffrey had been left behind in Windsor as part of the castle guard. Once she stopped probing for further information, he was able to relax and enjoy some time with Edith, now a beautiful twelve-year-old for whom a husband would soon need to be considered.

Hugh was ruefully asking himself which of the more eligible English nobles might still be infeft of their estates — or even still alive — for that purpose once John had wreaked his vengeance on the rebels, when Ranulf clattered into the manor courtyard. He was accompanied by several men at arms and announced that they were urgently summoned back to Nottingham, ahead of riding south to lift a siege.

'London?' Hugh asked. 'How can we possibly relieve an entire city with the few remaining loyal barons we have available?'

'Not London — Windsor,' Ranulf replied.

Hugh urgently hushed him in case they were overheard by Edwina. After a few kisses and hugs — and another torrent of complaints from Edwina that her husband had barely been home long enough to regain some of the weight he had lost — Hugh and Ranulf were back on the road.

Ten days later they sat on a slight rise just outside the village of Eton, along with the king, gazing down with trepidation at the ring of steel by which the royal palace of Windsor was now surrounded. Hugh and John were arguing over the predicted time they had available before those within its walls were starved into surrender when Ranulf gazed westwards towards the settlement that had recently established itself around Reading Abbey. Something flashed in the noonday sun. He gave a cry and pointed to a barely visible grey line on the distant horizon.

'If they are more rebels coming in from the west,' he called out, 'then we should be gone from here. There must be several thousand of them, by my mark.'

'We could take a stand against them here, on this hill,' John suggested.

Hugh gave a stifled groan. 'We might begin digging our graves while we wait, sire. Courage is one thing, but numbers are another, and there must be five of them for every one of us. I strongly recommend that we retreat.'

John looked behind him and snorted derisively. 'All around us is open ground, but at least up here we have the advantage of a hill defence of sorts. They would need to come at us up that slope, and this surely gives us an advantage.'

'That was the hope of the last Saxon king at Senlac Ridge, before your great-grandfather conquered England for Normandy,' Hugh reminded him. 'I believe that we should make haste back to Wallingford.'

'And I believe that we should show the scum no more weakness,' John retorted hotly. 'We stand our ground, and if necessary we die as brave heroes.'

'What say you, Ranulf?' Hugh asked in a desperate attempt to gain support for the strategic withdrawal that his military instincts were screaming out for.

Ranulf was preoccupied gazing towards the broad line of the approaching army. 'I remain unconvinced that they are more of the rebels,' he replied quietly after a moment's reflection. 'We know that the bulk of their force may be found in London, and that in the main their estates are north and east of here. Why, then, should so many be approaching from the west?'

'Perhaps Llywelyn of Wales has finally broken through the Marches,' John suggested.

Ranulf shook his head. 'When I was last in Chester, we got word that he was facing enemies closer to his far coast.'

'And in the main the Welsh are infantry armed with bows,' Hugh added, 'whereas the line approaching us is composed largely of men on horses.'

'We shall soon know their identities anyway,' John observed, 'since they appear to be travelling at speed, and their battle pennants are being flown in the vanguard.'

Ranulf squinted, then chuckled, and Hugh manoeuvred his horse alongside his cousin's as he muttered, 'Why does the prospect of your imminent death cause you such amusement?'

'Look more closely,' Ranulf whispered, 'but don't let John hear you. Take a look at those pennants — are they familiar?

Can you see the red lion rampant on a divided field of green and yellow, or have I lost either my wits or my eyesight?'

Hugh followed his gaze, and his jaw dropped. 'By God, you are right! Somehow you must persuade John that we need this man more urgently than the executioner does, while I go down to greet him.'

John looked angrily down at Hugh's retreating figure, then turned to Ranulf. 'If he is offering surrender terms, I shall have his head!'

'Far from it, sire,' Ranulf said. 'He brings the means of reclaiming your royal castle. If I might be so bold, do not give way to your natural and understandable anger when you see who Hugh brings into our fold.'

Hugh had reached the grizzled warrior seated three paces ahead of his men, on a massive warhorse that made Hugh's mount look like a lapdog. He bid him welcome.

'It has been a long time, but God grant that you come in peace.'

'I come with more than that,' the newcomer grinned down at him, 'but if John has his way, I may shortly depart in pieces.'

'There is little time to lose, if we are to regain Windsor before starvation forces them out,' Hugh replied, 'so waste no time in ceremony. John will bluster and rage, but underneath he is secretly afraid for his throne.'

'Ever the same John,' came the smiling reply. 'I shall leave it to you, as a seasoned man at arms, to persuade him that he needs the gift I bring him, on the terms I shall reveal.'

The man dismounted, and all six feet and more of him creaked up the slope in his chainmail, the visor down on his battle helm, until he stood before John and pulled it off to reveal the battle-scarred face underneath.

'Marshal the traitor!' John bellowed. 'Seize the man immediately, that he may answer for his treachery!'

'My answer is behind me,' William Marshal said confidently. 'All two thousand of them. Before you take the weight of my head from my shoulders, you might consider how best to employ them, bearing in mind that they answer only to my order.'

'You have brought them to my standard?' John asked in disbelief. 'Is this some ruse on the part of the barons to have me thrown from my determined course?'

'They are yours to command, John,' Marshal said. 'As I judge the situation, you might wish them to clear you a path into yon palace.'

'And *then* what?' John demanded, still suspicious.

'Then they are still yours, on two conditions,' Marshal replied. 'The first is that you cease calling me a traitor, when I am no such thing, and never have been. The second is that you release my son from the Tower, where he does not deserve to be. But in order to do that, of course, you will need to retake London, and it may be that I can assist in that also.'

'If you are no traitor, why did you flee to Ireland?' John demanded, but again Marshal had come equipped with a ready answer.

'I did not "flee" there. I merely found it advantageous to visit my Irish estates after you unjustly forfeited my Pembroke ones. Had I remained in Wales you would have had my head, and I would not be here now, offering you two thousand additional men at arms, many of them Irish and Welsh.'

'Has Llywelyn loaned you some of his knights?' John asked.

Marshal chuckled. 'In a manner of speaking. Given that he is currently in the dungeons of Pembroke Castle, he will have no immediate need of them.'

'You have put down the Welsh?' Hugh asked, clearly impressed.

Marshal nodded. 'The arrogant bastard thought to move into my estates in my absence, so I taught him a little respect. He is no longer a threat to England — unless I give orders for his release, or my wife does if I am executed as a traitor.'

'No more talk of treason, William,' said John. 'Your arrival is most gratifying, and you will prove both your undoubted valour and your loyalty to England if you chase the scum away from my royal residence. Then you may join us for supper.'

The rebels forming a ring around Windsor Castle took one look at the force that thundered towards them across the river meadows and departed in disarray, to rousing cheers and catcalls of disdain from Marshal's men. The castle servants rushed out of their hiding places to welcome back their king, and men were sent into Dorney Common to hunt for supper. Local merchants cautiously brought in wagonloads of fish and fowl, flour and ale, to the delight of the gate guards.

As they sat at supper, where Marshal was the obvious guest of honour, John turned to him with a frown.

'I shall not be able to order the release of your son until we have retaken London, William, and I can only hope that the rebels have not treated him unkindly.'

'Why would they?' Marshal said. 'They believe him to be the son of a traitor, and therefore someone aligned to their cause. But he is not the only son you should concern yourself about.'

'Your meaning?' John asked as he reached for another plum.

'My meaning is Louis of France, the young prince who is not only the son of your old enemy Philip, but also a cousin of sorts by marriage following his wedding to Blanche of Castile. He has ambitions to be King of England, and his father encourages him in that. The Pope, as you know, has excommunicated the father for his aggression towards you, but the son knows no such restraint, and the barons who oppose you have sent word across the Channel, inviting him to invade.'

'Dear God!' Hugh muttered, while Ranulf's face took on the appearance of a funeral mourner.

'That is the *real* reason why I am here,' Marshal continued. 'I may have cause to be aggrieved by the treatment of myself and my family by England's king, but I will *not* sit idly by while a young stripling strides like Alexander the Great over my native land. We must now begin to plan how best to resist this combined threat to what we cherish most about being Englishmen.'

The next week was spent almost entirely in a council of war in which the opinions of Marshal and Hugh won the day, given their lengthy combined experience of warfare. King Louis had landed unopposed in Kent, and John's first instinct had been to march south from Windsor to head him off before he succeeded in meeting up with the rebels in London. But the king finally accepted, with bad grace, that to do so would expose the royal forces, such as they were, to a pincer movement in which they would become trapped between the invading French and the marauding barons.

It was far better, they agreed, to retreat westwards, into estates that remained loyal to John. For one thing this would require the combined enemy to come to them, a tactic that would necessitate long supply lines that could be attacked. But more to the immediate point, they could build up their manpower by collecting men at arms from those nobles who could be persuaded that England should not become a mere outlying possession of a king based across the Channel, as it had been until the reign of John's father Henry — an age that many did not wish to see revived.

They began the retreat with great reluctance, given that it would almost certainly result in Windsor Castle once more falling into the hands of the rebel barons. But once they reached the Cotswolds and set up camp outside Tewkesbury, the volunteers came flooding in and the royal forces soon reached over four thousand in number. There were infantry, cavalry and a few specialists such as siege engineers, who Hugh took to organising into wings of the king's army that Marshal would lead. After two months in training, they looked back towards the north and east.

The rebels still held London and the counties to its south and east, and the battle plan that was eventually agreed by John was that they should skirt the north of London by way of Oxford until they reached Cambridge. Once they had command of this ancient town, they would effectively have cut the rebels off from their traditional estates, and therefore their most easily accessed supply lines.

Cambridge opened its gates to Marshal's forces, almost as if shamefaced regarding its role as a rebel recruiting base. After several hours of arguing, pleading, and even threatening to abandon the entire enterprise, Ranulf persuaded John not to exact revenge on its citizens. Instead, he was prevailed upon to attend a Divine Mass, to give thanks to God for delivering the town from his enemies.

Lincoln was the next target, since it was under siege from a detachment of Louis' army under the command of the Count of Perche, together with recruits from North Midlands rebel estates. The castle was still held in John's name by its castellan, who was, unusually, a woman. However, Nicola de la Haie was no ordinary woman, but a fiercely independent landholder of over a dozen surrounding estates. She was twice widowed, but had conducted herself so admirably in her joint roles of Constable of Lincoln and Sheriff of Lincolnshire that John had not thought to replace her with any Poitevin favourite. In truth he found her aggressive and resolute style attractive, although in private it was rumoured that he feared her.

Whatever her justification for leading the garrison at Lincoln, she was still firmly holding out against the Count of Perche, who had taken a serious risk in venturing so far north of the main French invading force. Hugh took early advantage of this by severing his supply line. He then obtained Marshal's blessing to lead a determined force of knights on horseback into the streets currently occupied by Frenchmen.

The town gates broke open under a sustained battering, while bowmen were sent onto rooftops to discharge volley after volley into the fleeing ranks. This left the streets empty of all but those of Perches' forces who had been ordered to ignore the rearguard attack and concentrate on continuing the siege. It fell quiet for several minutes while Hugh gathered his best horsemen into a tight-knit block, then gave the order to charge.

In the screaming, clashing melee that followed, the besieging forces broke in disarray, many of them heading for the south gate in an effort to escape; however, Marshal had anticipated this and had stationed detachments of Welsh foot soldiers just beyond each gate, who made quick work of the terrified and disorientated enemy as they fled for their lives.

It had been a complete rout, and only one stubborn knot of rebels remained under the castle walls. Hugh dismounted and commanded those of his men who remained uninjured to stalk towards the rebel group of fifty or so, in the hope of forcing them to flee. But their commander, hidden from sight beneath a battered helm, ordered them to remain, and the two groups came together in the familiar grinding clash of metal on metal.

It had been a long and active day, and Hugh was beginning to feel his age as he hacked wearily to his right and left, his sword arm feeling heavier every time he lifted it. He was also sweating profusely under his battle helm, and the sweat was beginning to blur his vision, which was probably why he failed to realise that he was surrounded. He also wasn't expecting the heavy blow from behind on the top of his helm, which felled him onto the blood-soaked ground as everything went black.

# XVII

Hugh opened his eyes when he felt the point of a sword at his throat, in the vulnerable space between the bottom of his helm and the top of his cuirass. The face that grinned down at him was only too familiar, although the circumstances were novel.

'You are fortunate that I was taught that the taking of prisoners is preferable to the wanton slaughter of your defeated opponent. So, Father, you are now my prisoner. Follow me,' Geoffrey instructed him as they remounted and rode swiftly back out through the north gate. 'They will not seek to intercept us while I have you prisoner, although it would seem that you have won the day. Once we are safely clear of the town itself, I will lower my sword.'

'How do you come to be fighting for the rebel cause?' Hugh asked, still attempting to absorb the events of the past few minutes.

Geoffrey grinned. 'I can blame you for that. Thanks to Uncle Robert, I found a safe hiding place on a farm in Clayworth, hard by Retford. Its tenant was one of those who was outlawed in the Shire Wood earlier in John's wicked occupation of Nottingham, in the days of the former King Richard. He was delighted to give sanctuary to someone who'd deserted John's service.'

'So you became a farmer?' Hugh said. 'However, it would seem that you never lost your skill as a knight.'

'A squire only,' Geoffrey corrected him. 'I'd been teaching the labourers on the farm the basics of swordplay, using tree branches for weapons just as I did in my youth, when the lord of the estate came recruiting. You've heard of Roger de Montbegon?'

'I've met him,' Hugh admitted as he recalled the man he'd threatened to throw out of Repton Manor. 'I assume that he's now among those who've taken up arms against King John?'

'He did so fairly early in the matter,' Geoffrey confirmed. 'When he returned from that signing ceremony near London, and the king appeared to be doing nothing to honour his undertaking, Roger joined the other rebels and began recruiting for an army to take into the field. He learned of my skill with arms, although he never knew my true identity. Anyway, he ordered me off the estate and back onto horseback, as a squire in his service. I served at Newark, Gainsborough, Ely and Cambridge, where we nearly met up again. Then we fell back on Lincoln, and you know the rest.'

'So where to now, assuming that I remain your prisoner?' Hugh asked, struck by the somewhat comical arrangement.

'I'm taking you back to Mother, where you'll be safe from your own foolhardiness in believing that a man approaching sixty years of age can still give a good account of himself on the battlefield.'

'And my ransom?'

'You already paid that, when you taught me skill in warfare,' Geoffrey said. 'Now, let's stop for a moment while I untie your wrists.'

'It will take at least three days to reach our manor house in Flint,' Hugh pointed out as they remounted and kept their horses' heads pointed westward along the track that would take them to Nottingham, 'so you have time to consider another option long before we reach there.'

'What, return to the land at Clayworth, you mean?'

'No, I mean return to the service of King John.'

'Never, after what I saw him do to those poor Welsh boys!' Geoffrey insisted.

'And you've never encountered worse on the battlefield?' Hugh challenged him. 'Brutality breeds brutality, and sometimes we commit deeds that our inner souls recoil from, simply in order to remain alive, or to make strategic gains.'

'Is this the same man who preached to me about showing mercy to a fallen opponent? The same mercy I showed to you back there in Lincoln?'

'That was, I hope, love for a father,' Hugh replied. 'The same father who may no longer be a strong fighting man, but who has the wisdom of years, and who can advise you that sooner or later John will prevail. If you are found in the rebel camp, you will die a horrible, and very public, death.'

'Surely I will anyway, once John lays eyes on me?'

'Three points,' Hugh replied quietly. 'The first is that it is better to die honourably, in battle, than to be executed as a traitor. The second is that you are now an experienced, battle-hardened man at arms, and John needs all that he can get. Thirdly, it is arrogance on your part to assume that John will remember you.'

'I can hardly go back there,' Geoffrey said with a backward jerk of his head, 'where I recently formed part of a rebel army.'

'You will not need to,' Hugh replied, 'since John was intending to march south to Lynn, in Norfolk, there to take on supplies from the Low Countries. We can be there in less time than it would take to go home, where John *would* think to find you, if not otherwise distracted. And your mother believes you to have been part of the guard inside Windsor Castle, which fell to the rebels again some weeks ago. If you insist on taking me back there, I may choose to tell her that she has a rebel for a son.'

'You do not believe that John will have me done to death?'

'Not for as long as you are part of my train, hidden beneath your battle helm.'

'And Uncle Ranulf — is he still part of your army?'

'He leads it, at least notionally. William Marshal is back amongst us, and John had more reason for taking his head than he ever did yours. He needs fighting men, not dead traitors.'

They approached Lynn cautiously. Hugh sought out Ranulf, to whom he recounted the recent turn of events before leading a nervous Geoffrey into the merchant's house that had been commandeered for Ranulf's temporary accommodation. John and William Marshal were installed in the Custom House overlooking the harbour.

'I had hoped to see you two again eventually,' Ranulf said as he embraced first Hugh, then Geoffrey, 'but I had not expected it to be so soon! You were fortunate that I recognised your captor, Hugh, because my men were all set to rescue you when they saw you being led away. Geoffrey would no doubt have been hacked down in the process. But what were you doing fighting for the rebels, you foolish boy?'

'Hardly a boy anymore,' Geoffrey frowned, 'and as for my motivation, you need look no further back than the slaughter of those hostages back in Nottingham. I could not serve a tyrant so cruel.'

'You would seem to have little choice at this moment,' Ranulf reminded him, 'unless the roles have been reversed, and you are now your father's prisoner.'

'John must not know that Geoffrey has returned,' Hugh urged him. 'There is a possibility that he may still remember him as a deserter. But in the meantime, he can hopefully advise us of the barons' plans. Other than inviting France to invade, of course.'

'Not just France,' Geoffrey told them. 'There was talk of support from both the Welsh and the Scots. Everyone, it seems, wishes to invade England.'

'As for the Welsh,' Ranulf said, 'their king has been confined in Pembroke Castle by William Marshal, who has rejoined John and been gratefully pardoned his perceived past treachery, not that he will admit to it.'

'Perhaps there is hope for Geoffrey, then,' Hugh suggested.

Ranulf shrugged. 'Not until he has proved his loyalty once again. In the meantime we must keep him hidden, then he may ride out as one of our company. Anyway, we are due to meet with John for supper in the Custom House, where he is carousing with William Marshal and celebrating the recapture of Lincoln. I think he wishes to head south again, to lift any siege of Windsor. Anyway, let's leave Geoffrey here and make our way into the presence.'

They were welcomed into the meeting hall by William Marshal, whose face was clouded with bad tidings. There was no sign of John at the table, and Ranulf raised one questioning eyebrow.

'He's in his garderobe, for the third time this afternoon,' William said. 'He claims it must have been a bad oyster from the banquet we had to celebrate our arrival here two days ago, but it may also have been caused by news of a northern invasion.'

'The Scots?' Ranulf asked.

Marshal nodded. 'You have heard?'

'I knew only from a rebel prisoner who we tortured for information,' Ranulf lied, 'and all he would disclose before he died was that the rebels had invited William of Scotland to invade from the north, and Llywelyn from the west. We know the fate of Llywelyn, but how far has the Scots king progressed?'

'He has already taken Carlisle, and is rumoured to have struck east into Northumbria. John plans to march north and cut him off before he can reach York.'

At that moment, a pale-faced John walked hesitantly through the door adjoining the rooms that had been commandeered as his private chambers. He smiled thinly as he helped himself to wine, then blanched as he looked down at the loaded supper table.

'Pray help yourselves to whatever takes your fancy, but avoid shellfish unless you wish to suffer the same affliction as myself. A little dry bread will suffice for me at this time, but we need to plot our journey north.'

'William has advised us of the Scots incursion,' Ranulf disclosed, 'and my best advice would be to drop south to Peterborough, then join the North Road to York, since it will give the fastest passage for your wagon train.'

'It's not the fastest route,' William argued. 'If we cut round the coast at Holbeach and strike north for Newark, we can join the same North Road a day's ride further north.'

'That means dragging a line of heavy wagons either across a long, sandy coastline, or slightly inland over one river course after another,' said Hugh. 'They don't call this the "Fenland" for nothing.'

'It's still quicker than these rough country roads,' William countered, 'and we save at least a day by my route.'

'Sort it out among yourselves,' John groaned as he rose from the table, clutching his guts and making a hasty retreat through the adjoining door.

'A pity about the shellfish,' Ranulf said unsympathetically, 'since I've always been partial to crays.'

William was able to persuade John that his would be the better route. Shortly after sunrise two days later, the royal progress rumbled out of the town by way of the south gate and along the south bank of the mighty River Ouse. John was being carried in a litter ahead of the baggage train, and was surrounded by not only men at arms but also the royal physician, who called a halt every few minutes in order to disappear inside the litter curtain and emerge with a pot that he then emptied at the side of the road. From time to time, groans could be heard from the litter, and the physician urged the carter on the litter horse to avoid ruts in the track as far as possible.

Hugh had been assigned the duty of guarding the wagons, along with thirty or so of his mounted men at arms that included Geoffrey, because of their valuable contents that were transported wherever John went. Ranulf and William Marshal rode at the head of the vanguard. As they approached Wisbech in the Isle of Ely, Ranulf rode back to where Hugh and Geoffrey were patrolling up and down the wagons. Alongside him was the physician, and Ranulf explained that John was too ill to proceed on such a bumpy route. The physician wished him to be taken urgently to a nearby holy house, where there might be monks with the necessary potions to ease his worsening flux.

'We are advised by one of the wagoners, who is from these parts, that there is an abbey up ahead at Swineshead,' the physician added, 'and we must lose no time in reaching it, if we are to ease His Majesty's suffering.'

'But he has given orders that the wagons are to proceed with all possible speed to Newark, where he will meet up with you once he has recovered his strength and rested,' Ranulf added. 'William is still insisting that his chosen route is the swiftest.'

'That's because he doesn't have to haul baggage wagons along it,' Hugh grumbled. 'But we shall do as ordered. Remember me to my wife if we finish up with the fish in one of these murky outlets.'

'Don't be tempted to eat any of the shellfish, unless you want to die more swiftly and messily,' the physician instructed him as he turned his horse's head and headed back towards the royal litter.

Hugh sighed and turned to Geoffrey. 'We may have to swim for it at some stage, but an order is an order, however ridiculous. Remember that the coronation regalia are in one of these wagons, so don't lose sight of them.'

An hour later they came to a small village called Sutton Bridge, and ahead of them was a seemingly endless tract of marshy silt beds, with abundant wildfowl that rose, screaming, into the air at their approach. There was a narrow track of sorts visible through this wasteland, and Hugh ordered the first of the wagons onto it without delay. The carter grumbled, but did as he was told, and one by one the heavily laden carts made their way onto the slightly raised walkway. Geoffrey was ordered ahead to urge the leading wagon master to make as much speed as he could. Meanwhile, Hugh dropped back to the rear and advised the man at the reins of the final wagon that he would need to wait for a brief while until the loads ahead of him had lumbered their way north.

As Hugh sat to one side, wondering how anyone might survive in order to make a living in this wet and dismal wasteland, the sky began to darken, and rain clouds lowered from the west. A sheet of soaking misery then descended, adding to their discomfort and reducing their ability to see what lay before them. But finally the cart ahead jerked forward, and Hugh signalled for the final baggage wagon to follow.

A few minutes later he became aware of a new hazard that he had not been able to spot earlier due to the reduced visibility. The track ahead was lying in several inches of salty water that flowed slowly but relentlessly from right to left. Given that the sea was somewhere to their right, one did not need to be a sailor to realise that the ocean was slowly coming in, and that this entire stretch of land must be tidal. He barely had time to wonder how far the leading wagon had got when he heard a curse from the man on the final wagon, whose wheels had become bogged as the ground beneath them softened.

Hugh dismounted quickly and ordered the carter down from his front board. Between them they managed to lift the wheels out of the squelching, sucking mud, and the wagoner ran forward and smacked the horse into a lurching forward motion. This happened three more times in the space of half an hour, before they were obliged to halt because the wagon ahead of theirs was even more securely bogged than their own.

From further ahead could be heard shouts, curses and pleas for help, all of them delivered in a high pitch that denoted panic. The water was now up to Hugh's knees, and he stepped to his left in the hope of finding higher ground. Instead, he felt himself sinking into a deep pit of silty ooze, and when he tried to free one leg it remained firmly where it was. His efforts to free it caused him to sink down to his waist. With a jolt of alarm he recognised it for what it was, since the Dee estuary on his own estate was renowned for it. It had a name that struck terror into the hearts of those who went in search of shellfish: quicksand.

His brain told him that any attempt to struggle would only result in him sinking more quickly into a bottomless pit that would eventually cover his head and suffocate him. It was now almost totally dark, and the wagon master who'd been by his side was splashing away somewhere back on the track, cursing and praying as he tried to go back the way he had come. It was useless to call for help, since the man was intent on saving his own life, and who could blame him? Instead, Hugh occupied his mind in sending loving thoughts back to Flint, to the devoted wife and beautiful daughter who would mourn his passing. At least Geoffrey would be able to relate the circumstances of it, assuming that he had made it safely to the other end of this marshy graveyard.

He assumed that he'd begun to hallucinate when he heard Geoffrey's voice calling his name, then came alert again as a heavy splashing noise heralded the arrival of a horseman. He looked up with a wan smile as he recognised the son who had been occupying his thoughts, then realised that he too was in danger. 'Come no closer!' he called to Geoffrey. 'Quicksand! Leave me to my fate, and save yourself!'

'Mother bade me keep an eye on you when we rode out together to visit Wales,' Geoffrey replied as he hastily dismounted into three feet of rising water, 'and I fear to answer to her if I fail to do so. Grab this halter rope when I throw it to you, and for God's sake don't miss it!'

The rope came curling out of the oily darkness, and Hugh grabbed it, dimly aware that Geoffrey had climbed back onto his horse and was tying the other end of the halter rope to the bridle. Then Geoffrey dug his spurs sharply into the flanks of the mount, which gave a loud whinny of protest and reared up. Hugh felt a bone-jarring jerk all the way down from his shoulders to the soles of his boots, and suddenly he had broken free of the vice-like grip of the quicksand, and was lying flat on his face in four feet of water. He felt urgent hands pulling him upright by his shoulders, and was then commanded to throw himself onto the neck of the stomping and snorting horse as Geoffrey pulled its head round and urged it into a canter back towards Sutton Bridge.

After what seemed like an hour, Hugh was lying on his back on a grassy slope in the darkness, and Geoffrey was comforting and praising his exhausted mount. The cries from the marsh were getting fainter in the impenetrable darkness, and Hugh recited one of the few prayers of thanks that he could remember from his childhood days under a tutor who had also been a clergyman.

He saw Geoffrey's enquiring face looking down into his, and he nodded.

'I'm alive, but wet, thanks to you.'

'You got wet on your own account,' Geoffrey said, 'but I'll take credit for saving your life. You might want to put in a good word for me with the king — after you explain how you came to lose almost his entire baggage train to the incoming ocean.'

# XVIII

Ranulf rushed out to meet them as they wound their way wearily up the steep grass slope towards the gatehouse of Newark Castle. Hugh was astride a horse he had acquired in Wisbech, which he would be thoroughly glad to stop riding.

'Thank God you survived!' Ranulf yelled. 'There are tales being told that most of the baggage train was lost, along with the men who were guarding it.'

'They are largely true,' Hugh admitted, 'and I would have become one of the lost, had it not been for Geoffrey, yet again. You really should get yourself some sons, Ranulf.'

'So the royal baggage is lost?' Geoffrey asked.

Ranulf nodded. 'All but two wagons that contained Exchequer Rolls. But the coronation jewels must be somewhere on the ocean floor.'

'The king will have my head!' Hugh groaned.

'You clearly have not yet heard,' said Ranulf. 'John lies close to death in a chamber upstairs that reeks of decay and despair. The flux has worsened, and he excretes more by the minute than he ever did in a month. There is talk of poison, but whatever the cause he is very weak, and the physician has sent for the archbishop to give him his final rites.'

'I wonder if God will grant him entry into Heaven,' Geoffrey murmured.

Hugh turned quickly to admonish him. 'Keep your thoughts to yourself, Geoffrey — you may have saved my life twice, but I could not preserve yours if you were heard saying such things in the wrong quarter.'

'Talking of quarters,' Ranulf interjected, 'mine are above the bakehouse. They are noisy, but warm, and there should be room for two more pallets in there. John is on the first floor of the Tower, and as you can see there is little to be had in the way of accommodation. I am only here because I'm assisting Marshal in the guard duties. Or, at least, my men are. It is unlikely that John will ever leave here, so we'll have time enough to travel home before the entire nation collapses, and we can go and hide.'

'I refuse to give up that easily,' Hugh insisted. 'Even without John, there will be a king to serve. He has a son, does he not?'

'He has five offspring in all, but only two sons. The elder — Henry — is only nine. The barons will no doubt seize the moment, so let us seize *this* moment to eat,' Ranulf said as he pointed in the direction of their quarters. 'The kitchens bake three times a day, so we might manage to get some bread without weevils in. But if you were hoping for meat, you will be disappointed. It goes without saying that we have all foresworn fish, but the local cheese is well worth investigation.'

They were halfway through forcing down day-old bread with lashings of honey when a monk appeared in the doorway of their humble chamber.

'His Grace of Canterbury seeks your attendance in the king's sickness chamber,' he announced, before bowing backwards and disappearing as stealthily as he had appeared. Hugh rose to his feet, but Ranulf remained where he was.

'I have not yet eaten my fill, and there may be nothing by tomorrow, so please take your seat again,' he said. 'Then, when we are ready, we must call in at the kitchens.'

'Surely, even you will have eaten enough by then?' Hugh said.

Ranulf nodded. 'That is not what I had in mind.'

A short while later Hugh hung back at the kitchen door while Ranulf spoke quietly to the Cook, then came back holding two oranges with their tops cut off. He handed one to Hugh, and the other he retained for himself.

Hugh sniffed his suspiciously, then recoiled from the pungent fumes that it gave off.

'Vinegar,' Ranulf said. 'They say it has the power to ward off evil humours, but more to the point it masks bad smells. And believe me, where we are headed smells *very* bad indeed.'

'Oranges would seem to be in season,' John observed in a rasping voice from where he lay swaddled in bedclothes. A physician was attempting to get him to swallow more of a vile-looking green 'simple', while those around the bed made valiant efforts to avert their eyes from the crumpled remains of the man who seemed destined not to be their king for much longer.

'Now that you are all gathered,' John continued as if apprehensive that his voice was about to desert him, 'there are certain orders I wish to give. My physician, ever a simpering old fool, tells me that I am not long for this life. In case he is correct — for once — then there are certain arrangements that I must make. Should I live, I will of course revoke them, but for the moment listen carefully.'

It fell silent for a moment, then John made a determined effort to raise his head from the bolster, only to sink back again with a groan. After several attempts to take deep breaths that were painful to listen to, he went on.

'First, the succession. There can be no doubt, I hope, that Prince Henry is to succeed me. However, he is still only nine years old, and will require a Regency Council to govern in his name until he attains his majority. William, I see you lurking there in the shadows. Onto you I devolve the task of forming that Council, choosing whomsoever you deem it best to appoint, although I wish the tutoring of the boy in matters of kingship to be allocated to my good friend Peter des Roches, the Bishop of Winchester. Do you accept that solemn office?'

'With all my heart, sire,' Marshal replied, 'but pray God that I shall not be required to don that mantle for many years to come.'

John replied with a harsh chuckle that provoked a bout of liquid coughing and an ominous noise from between the bedding that several pages hastily moved forward to rectify, while oranges were raised to faces. When he recovered John called out for Ranulf, who edged forward into the king's line of vision.

'My dear friend and trusted ally the Earl of Chester, who has never once deserted me, despite the treachery of others. You are ennobled beyond reckoning, thanks largely to me, so there would be little point in granting you a new earldom. However, there has been much bickering, among those who deserve only death for treason, over the lands of Leicester that have been wanting a lord since the death of Robert de Beaumont. Since one of the claimants is of the traitorous de Montfort brood who helped King Philip regain Normandy, I would not sleep comfortably in my grave should it go to them. I therefore invest you with the whole of the Leicester inheritance, to do with as you wish. You may even assume the title of "Earl of Leicester", should you wish, but at least the wealth that comes with the estates should serve as a fitting reward for your loyal services to England.'

'I fear you are too generous, sire,' Ranulf murmured.

John nodded. 'So do I, but where I am bound it will not matter. Now, where is your able master at arms the Earl of Flint?'

'Here, sire,' Hugh announced as he stepped forward to stand alongside Ranulf.

John smiled. 'Time for you to be put out to grass, I think, Hugh. You have almost managed to lose your life several times in the royal service, and it is only a matter of time before you succeed. A man of over sixty years of age has no right to be wearing chainmail, unless he is William Marshal. Although I have no doubt that you will disobey me yet again, I hereby discharge you from your martial duties, with a pension of five hundred marks a year. Go back to your wife and children, and advise your disobedient oaf of a son that he is pardoned for deserting my service in Nottingham.'

'My grateful thanks, sire,' Hugh murmured as he felt the tears of gratitude rising in his throat at the thought of finally returning home.

John gave up his struggle for life in the early hours of the following morning, during a violent thunderstorm that many took to be an expression of God's anger at the late king's presumption in presenting himself at Heaven's gates. The small, devoted group that had gathered around his deathbed dispersed in various directions. It was left to William Marshal to accompany the body down to Worcester Cathedral, where John had asked to be buried.

Edith of Flint looked up from her seat in the sun, then threw her needlework down into the grass as she called loudly through the open door of the manor.

'Mother, we have visitors! And *such* visitors! I shall need a new coif for the banquet if Father is bringing me a suitor at last. Oh no, I see that it's only my brother.'

'*Only* your brother?' Edwina chided her as she raced out from the house and stood breathlessly awaiting the moment when the two men dismounted. 'God be praised!'

As the groom led both horses to the stables, she ran forward to embrace her husband and son. Then she stepped back and looked admiringly at them both.

'You are both alive and intact, which is more than either of you deserve, but I shall light a candle to the Blessed Virgin nevertheless. And how long do you intend to stay *this* time?'

'For myself, this is probably my final homecoming,' Hugh beamed, 'since John discharged me from the royal service shortly before his death, and the Regent William Marshal does not require a man as old as himself to fight his battles. But Geoffrey — who you should know has saved my life twice since we last left here — will be taking up duties as the Constable of Chester Castle. Ranulf has become Earl of Leicester as well as Earl of Chester, and he insisted that he could not turn his mind to managing his newly acquired Midland estates without assurance that his back was adequately guarded further north.'

'Edith, please tell Cook to prepare a lavish dinner with the best meats that she has available,' Edwina instructed. She then led Hugh by the hand further down the path and into the rose walk to the side. They sat on the bench holding hands like young lovers, as Edwina began demanding answers to all the questions that were racing through her mind. 'You say that John is dead? Who, then, will rule the nation? Those rebellious barons?'

'Not if William Marshal has his way,' Hugh laughed lightly. 'He is appointed Regent for the young heir Henry, and has vowed to bring the rebels to heel before they have time to realise what has happened.'

'But you swear that he has not demanded your services?'

'He has not, so settle your mind that I am home for good. I offered to serve under him, and he rejected that offer in terms that were almost insulting. I am too old to fight, apparently.'

'I can only agree with that,' Edwina said as she poked him playfully in his rounded stomach. 'But what did you mean about Geoffrey saving your life on two occasions?'

'More about that once we have eaten, and Geoffrey is present in order to lap up the praise before he heads back to Chester, where Ranulf has made him castellan.'

Edwina sighed. 'At least I have one of you back for good. We can only hope that England settles into a long period of peace — God knows it deserves it. It seems that my whole life has been consumed by fighting between members of the same family. Is it now at an end, think you?'

Hugh gazed out towards the shimmering haze above the Dee Estuary. 'Who can tell? Prince Henry comes from a long line of bad-tempered, over-ambitious and unforgiving tyrants. There may be more unrest yet to come.'

# A NOTE TO THE READER

Dear Reader,

Thank you for taking the time to read this sixth novel in a series of seven that between them cover the twelfth century, a period during which England was transformed beyond recognition. I hope that it lived up to your expectations. Once again, the basic plotline was written for me by the events that really happened during another of the many unsettled periods of that age.

Those who only studied England's history — often unwillingly — at school will probably only remember three things about King John. The first is that he was 'bad', the second is that he signed the Magna Carta, and the third is that he lost his jewels in the Wash. None of these three generalised assertions is entirely accurate.

First of all, he was 'bad' only to those who displeased him, or rebelled against his rule. To those who remained loyal to him, he was perhaps over-generous. One of the sources of the barons' discontent, leading to the Magna Carta, was that he enjoyed foreign favourites, particularly from Poitou, one of the few remaining Angevin estates across the Channel after John's lamentable loss of Normandy.

His appalling military judgment was another source of English baronial resentment, along with the taxation policies that were employed in order to finance John's almost quixotic attempts to regain English estates lost to Philip of France. The barons did not rebel because John was 'bad' *per se*; it was more the case that he was not 'good' at serving English hopes and aspirations.

Today, with the benefit of hindsight and a knowledge of how our constitutional rights developed over the subsequent centuries, it is tempting to regard 'The Great Charter' as the first keystone of civil liberties, a guarantee of freedom from arbitrary punishment. But seen in its context, it was the limited response of a group of nobles who were not prepared to cough up any more in the way of scutage tax, or lose their family estates because they refused to bring men to the royal battle standard. And for the record, John did not 'sign' the Magna Carta, since that was not the way it was done in those days. His acceptance was signified by the application of the royal seal, for all that was worth.

It's doubtful if John ever intended to honour the Charter even when he was affixing his seal to it, but his blatant, almost jubilant, failure to do so provoked the final military uprising during which John lost his life — not on the battlefield, but at the dinner table. 'A surfeit of peaches' was the line we were fed at school, but given the hygiene standards in Medieval kitchens, it could have been anything that caused the fatal dysentery. My choice of bad shellfish is as good a guess as any.

And finally, the loss of the Crown Jewels. As a child at school, hearing the oft-repeated line about the circumstances of that loss, I formed a somewhat bemused mental picture of a king misplacing his jewels of State among his socks and underwear in the royal laundry, until I came to learn that 'the Wash' is an area of eastern England that looks as if a hungry Viking giant bit a large chunk out of it.

In the main it is still swampy wetland, a treacherously tidal wildfowl sanctuary that is dangerous to cross, given its patches of quicksand and its ever-changing inlets. Imagine a long line of crude, heavy, twelfth-century baggage wagons being led across it by carters unfamiliar with the topography, and it is easy to see how they came to grief. The official records are scanty on the actual fate of the royal regalia, worth an estimated seventy million in modern money, but it's perhaps significant that when the boy king Henry, John's son, was hastily crowned a week after John's death, he was obliged to borrow a coronet from his mother to substitute for the lost Crown of State.

Henry's accession was followed by a lengthy period of unrest in the nation, while warring nobles jostled for pre-eminence. The Magna Carta remained unhonoured, and Henry was forced into signing a new and improved version of it that he also ignored. The barons who rebelled this time were led by another famous but shadowy figure from English Medieval history, Simon de Montfort, and he is the focus of the seventh, and final, novel in this series.

I hope that you are sufficiently encouraged to acquire the next instalment, but whether you are or not, I'd love to get feedback from you on this one — or perhaps even a review of it on **Amazon** or **Goodreads**. Or, if you prefer, send your thoughts to me on my author website, **davidfieldauthor.com**.

David

SAPERE
BOOKS

Printed in Great Britain
by Amazon

17428946R00122